SPIES, LIES, & CUPCAKES

(REBELS & MISFITS DETECTIVES, #1)

JESSICA SORENSEN

LUNA

I HAVEN'T ALWAYS KNOWN my parents were crazy. It took a few defining moments to make me fully aware of it. One of the biggest ones was when I made friends for the first time. It was way back in grade school, and they're still my friends now. But anyway, that's not really the point. The point is that when I made friends and listened to them talk about their lives at home, I realized something wasn't quite right at mine.

Take for instance right now. I'm standing in the backyard and my mom is urging me to burn all of my clothes.

"I want you to light them on fire." She urges the matches and lighter fluid toward me. "You should be the one to do this. It was your mistake."

I stare at my clothes, jewelry, and a few pairs of heels piled on the back lawn. "I can't."

"Luna, this isn't up for debate. You will burn these clothes. They're too immodest. I can't believe you bought them." She points a finger at the pile of clothes. "Those shorts are too short, and don't even get me started on the skirts. They don't even go to your knees. Our rules are no skirts unless they go to your knees. You know that, so why would you wear it? What's wrong with you?" She shakes her head. "Your father and I taught you to be better than this." She eyes the skinny jeans and black T-shirt I'm wearing. "Maybe we should burn those jeans, too. They look really tight."

I used to think this was normal behavior. Now, though...

"These jeans are fine, mom," I say, wishing I could stand up for myself once.

I wish I could say a lot of things to her. That her standards are too high. That I don't think I'll ever be the perfect, proper, church going daughter she wants me to be. I'm nowhere near perfect. Some of the stuff I've done … They'd probably lock me up if they knew everything about me.

"I'm not going to argue with you." She smooths invisible wrinkles from her turtleneck sweater. It's eighty degrees outside; she has to be sweating to death. But that's how she always dresses, like she's afraid to show even an inch of skin. "After what you did last weekend, you're lucky you're getting off this easy."

Easy? Is she kidding me? This is not easy at all. Being grounded is any easy punishment. Heck, I'd take getting locked up in my room over this.

But I know my mom well enough to understand that she isn't going to back down from this. So, sighing, I grab the lighter fluid and box of matches from her hand and turn to the pile of clothes. The smell of the lighter fluid makes me gag as I douse my beautiful skirts and shorts I've secretly been wearing over the last year.

My beautiful clothes. I miss them already. And I know that might make me sound as crazy as my parents, but they were really the only things that were me. And I'd always careful not to wear them any place my mom might see me. I'd change into the outfits at school or at one of my friends' houses then change back before I returned home. But last weekend, I was at one of the few parties I've gone to when the cops showed up and forced everyone to call their parents. I didn't have an extra set of clothes with me, so not only did my parents have to come and pick me up from a party, but they saw me in the black dress I had on. And let's just say she wasn't happy at all. But you probably got that already, considering I'm about to light my clothes on fire.

Burning them is my punishment, and my mom also put a tracking app on my phone so she can keep tabs on me. It's not the first time she has done this, and I'm guessing it won't be the last.

"Now the match," my mom says after I've soaked the clothes with lighter fluid.

Gritting my teeth, I pluck a match out of the box, strike the tip against the side, and drop it onto the pile. As the clothes erupt in flames, I have to look away. I stare down at the burn scars on my hands, struggling not to cry.

I got the scars when I was younger and our house caught on fire. I can't remember much about what happened, but sometimes, when I'm dreaming, I see myself in a bedroom, about to be burned alive.

"This is for the best." My mom's expression sharpens when she notes I'm looking at my scars. "Luna, get over it. We're outside, in the backyard. The house isn't going to burn down." She huffs an aggravated breath when I don't look up then cups my chin with her fingers, forcing me to meet her gaze. "This little phase you've been going through is going to end. Fitting in isn't what's important in life. As long as you live under my roof, you will obey our rules. You will wear clothes I pick out for you. You will never, ever wear a dress or any outfit like that again."

I smash my lips together, biting back words that will get my butt in trouble even more. She doesn't get it. Changing the way I dress isn't about fitting in. It's about being myself.

My parents have always been strict with me. They have hardcore beliefs about how people should behave and dress, and I'm expected to live up to those standards. Their beliefs aren't the only reason they're so strict, though. A lot of it has to do with how they were raised.

My grandparents on both sides are extremely intense. They frequently lecture my mom and dad on ways they need to improve not only themselves, but me, too. My parents act just like their parents do and have similar rules. There is no cursing allowed, only PG movies are permitted, and Sundays are spent at church. I have to wear clothes my mom picks out, no makeup ever, and no dating unless she approves of the guy. My mom has only ever approved of one guy. He goes to our church and is about as boring as watching paint dry.

I went out on one date with him and was completely miserable. When I came home and told my mom I didn't want to see him again, she said, "You're expecting too much. Dating isn't supposed to be fun. It's supposed to be an opportunity to find a person to marry and start a family with. That's how things worked with your father and me."

Yeah... I didn't know how to respond to that. I'm only a senior in high school, and marriage and starting a family are the last things on my mind. What about graduating? College? They never seemed to care about that sort of stuff.

Things have been this way for as long as I can remember. I've never had control over my life, never had the chance to be my own person. I've never had the freedom to explore who I am, what I like, what I want.

What I do know about myself is that I sure as hell don't want to stay home after I graduate and wait for a future husband my parents approve of to put a ring on my finger and knock me up. I want to finally be able to explore who I am.

The outfits burning on the lawn are a step in that direction, my way to find out what *I* like. But in the back of my mind when I was wearing each outfit, I heard a voice whispering that what I was doing was wrong. I heard the voice every time I did something rebellious, and the voice sounded like my mother's.

"You don't want to turn out like your aunt Ashlynn, do you?" she asks as the fire simmers and hisses.

Whenever I screw up, she throws Aunt Ashlynn into the mix. She's what the Harveys consider the bad seed of the family. I haven't seen her since I was four years old and hardly remember anything about her, yet I feel like I know her since she's constantly used as an example of who not to be.

I almost reply yes and tell my mom that I want to be just like Aunt Ashlynn. But the fear of getting kicked out of the house stops me. While I want to move out on my own, my parents won't allow me to get a job, so I have no money, no place to live, no nothing.

"No, I don't," I say, watching the flames blaze higher.

"Good, because after the stunt you pulled, I was starting to wonder if it was time to give up on you," she says coldly.

Maybe it's because I don't think I can do this anymore.

Silence stretches between us as the fire crackles, singeing the clothes and melting the jewelry.

Again, I look down at the jagged, elevated scars that cover my palms. Considering my history with fires, you'd think my mom would've picked a different punishment. But, no, that's not her style. She likes to punish to the max and make me as uncomfortable as she can.

"I need to go pick up a few things from the store for a school project," I lie, backing away from the fire.

"Take your phone with you so I can see where you are at all times," my mother shouts as I slide open the back door of the house. "You're on thin ice. If you keep heading in this direction, then ..." She trails off, turning back to the fire. "This punishment will seem like a piece of cake."

I step inside the house and shut the door, wanting to scream until my lungs explode. I want to shout that I'm not a bad person.

But I don't.

Nah, that's not my style of outlet.

No, mine is much more subtle.

Way, way more subtle.

LUNA

By the time I park in front of Benny and Gale's Corner Store, the sun is setting behind the shallow hills. Soon, the entire town will close up for the evening. That's how things work in Ridgefield. It has a 50s, small town, homey, good neighbor vibe.

Tourists who drive through here during the summer are always raving about what a fantastic town it is and how wonderful the people are. But I've grown up here, and not everything is how it appears. Like every other place in the world, the people who live in Ridgefield have secrets kept hidden behind locked doors. Sometimes, the occasional secret slips out and ends up printed in the news, like the time Mable Marleinton got arrested for drug possession and assault.

I have secrets, too. Mine have remained a secret, though. Thankfully or else burning my clothes in the backyard would look like a treat.

"Hey, Luna," Benny, the owner, greets me as I enter the store. "What are you doing out this late?"

I contain a sigh. Late? It's not even past six o'clock.

"My mom needs me to pick up some last minute stuff for a brunch party she's having tomorrow," I lie.

His warm smile makes me feel a pang of guilt over what I'm about to do.

"Tell her I said hi, okay?" he says as he punches a few buttons on the register. "I haven't seen her for a couple of weeks."

"I will," I tell him then hurry down the nearest aisle.

I tie my hoodie around my waist and wander up and down the aisles, trying to figure out what I'm going to buy for the fake brunch party. I decide on some paper plates and cups with smiley face hearts on them. Then I veer down the makeup aisle and eye the section of brightly colored nail polish.

My mom would lose her mind if I painted my nails a bold color like luscious purple or seductive red. I don't even like red or purple that much, but just the thought of her telling me I can't paint my nails makes me want to.

What if I did do it? What if I said to hell with her rules and did whatever I wanted? What would she do? Probably get rid of me like she did Mr. Buttons, a puppy I found on my way home from school. My mom thought he was the cutest puppy in the world until he pooped on the carpet and chewed up a favorite pair of shoes after weeks of trying to train him. Then it was bye-bye, Mr. Buttons.

Is that where I'm heading? Is my mom going to kick my ass out the door like she did with Mr. Buttons?

Do I care?

Le sigh. Why can't she just accept me for who I am? Why can't I act how I want without feeling guilty?

Nearly bursting with frustration, I snatch up some bottles of nail polish and stuff them into the pocket of my hoodie. For a second, I feel calm, like I have control over something. Then the images of my clothes on fire flash through my mind, and those invisible fingers wrap around my neck. Struggling not to scream, I start stuffing random items into my pocket one after the other. I'm not even paying attention to the items I'm picking up. Usually, I'm more careful, but today has been over-whelming, and I can't seem to think about anything except my clothes.

They're just clothes, I keep telling myself. But they weren't just clothes. They represented the time I spent finding my place in the world. And now it's all gone. Where does that leave me? Back to being my mom and dad's puppet? Back to dressing how they want me to, only listening to music they approve of, going to church, spending at least three hours a day working on homework even when I don't have anything to work on?

Sure, I have to do most of those things already, but being able to dress how I want gives me room to breathe.

I'm so frustrated that I feel like banging my head against the wall. Instead, I add more items into my pocket, growing more furious by the second. I'm losing it. I know I am. And I'm not being careful, something I become aware of as I realize I'm not alone.

Standing down the aisle with his eyes trained on me is Grey Sawyer.

I freeze with a hand-caught-in-the-cookie-jar look on my face.

Well, crap.

Grey is one of those guys who is nearly perfect. Well, in terms of looks. His brown hair looks so soft, and he has these incredibly blue eyes. Plus, he's taller than me, which is rare considering I'm almost five-foot-eleven.

I used to have a crush on him—still do when I'm being honest with myself. Normally, I'd dance up and down that he's staring at me so intently. Right now, though, I wish he'd leave.

Walk away, beautiful boy. Walk away.

Instead, he keeps his eyes on me and cocks a brow,

like he can't read my mind. Which clearly he can't since mindreading powers don't exist. But wouldn't it be cool if they did?

Unfortunately, they don't, though, and panic slams through me. How long has he been watching me? Maybe I should ask him. Just say, *Hey, did you just see me jack, like, ten items from sweet old Benny?* On top of that conversation being awkward, Grey and I aren't in the same social circles, and I don't know him well enough to guess how he'd react. All I really know about him, aside from the fact that he's been blessed with the gorgeous gene, is he's popular and has a bunch of friends who constantly make fun of people. He sometimes joins in with them and acts like an asshole, but he has been quieter this school year.

It's strange to see him as the more reserved guy he's pretending to be. I've witnessed him be a cocky little shit several times, like during sophomore year when I asked him to go to the Girl's Choice Dance. It took all of my courage to ask him, and all he did was give me a once-over and tell me no fucking way. Then, two days later, he said yes to Cindy Pepperson, a pretty, popular cheerleader. That's when I realized he had a type, and I didn't fit the criteria. I also realized I needed to pull my head out of my butt and get over my crush.

The worst part about the whole thing is he told the entire school about the dorky, prude girl who asked him out, and I was mocked for an entire year. Back then, I was different, though. Back then, I still wore outfits approved by my mom … okay, which I guess I kind of do now. But only until I get new clothes. And just because I'm back to wearing my old clothes doesn't mean I'm the old Luna. I'm stronger than I used to be.

Not that that strong girl isn't above bailing right now, though.

I start to back away from Grey, figuring it might be better to make a run for it. You know, just take off and bail. I doubt he'd chase me down. I don't think so anyway.

As I'm creeping away like a skittish rodent, his head slants to the side as a mixture of curiosity and concern rises in his expression.

I pause. *What the heck is that look for?*

"Did you find everything you needed for your mom's party?" Benny appears at the end of the aisle.

"Um… Yep." I hold up the paper cups and plates I'm carrying as I peek over at Grey, wondering if he'll rat me out to Benny.

Grey's expression is neutral and completely unreadable, and again, I find myself wishing mindreading powers existed.

What the hell is he thinking?

"Luna, I need to talk to you." Benny throws a swift glance in Grey's direction, and then his eyes land on me.

"Could you come to the front of the store with me, please?"

Oh. My. God. He knows.

God. No. No. No. This can't be happening.

Vomit burns at the back of my throat as I nod.

Benny motions for me to follow him and heads down the aisle.

My adrenaline soars as I trail after him. What am I going to do? My parents are going to kick me to the street if they find out I've been shoplifting. Do I have time to empty out everything from my pocket? Maybe I can fake trip, knock everything over on a shelf, then drop all the stuff inside my pocket onto the floor.

Am I that stealthy?

Yeah, probably not. And knowing my luck, I'd end up not knocking stuff off the shelf, and instead, face planting it onto the floor.

Well, I guess it's time to face the music, Luna. I hope you got your fill of sunshine and fresh air because it'll probably be the last time you ever get to see and breathe it.

As I squeeze past Grey, he reaches out and discreetly but quickly tugs my jacket off my waist.

"What are you doing?" I hiss as he puts on the over-sized grey jacket like it's his own.

Before Grey can answer, Benny twists around with a stern look on his face. "Luna, I need to see you now, please."

"Um... Yeah... Okay." I hurry away from Grey, but I can feel his eyes boring a hole into the side of my head.

Once we make it up front to the register, Benny instructs me to empty out my pockets, and I do what he asks, taking out my cell phone, a pack of gum, and a ten-dollar bill.

Puzzlement etches his face as he sorts through my stuff then looks down at my waist, his confusion deepening.

I hold my breath, waiting for him to say something.

"I'm so sorry, Luna," he says, running his hand over his bald head. "I thought maybe ... You know what, never mind. I think I'm losing my mind in my old age."

"It's okay." I feel like a total asshole.

I hurry and pay for the paper plates and cups then bolt out the door and back to my car. By the time I turn on the engine, my heart is pounding so hard I swear it's going to give out on me.

I'm the worst person in the world. I really am. And now Grey knows it I am. Even my closest friends don't know I've been shoplifting for years. Not because I need the stuff, but because, for some messed up reason, it gives me a sense of control.

I consider waiting until Grey comes out of the store to get my jacket back. I could ask him why he did what he did—why he helped me out—and if he plans on telling anyone about it. But when I see him exit the store with my jacket on, I chicken out and hide in my car.

"This is so messed up. How the hell do I handle this situation?" What I would give to have an answer to that.

But if I knew how to handle situations in my life, I might not be in this situation to begin with.

LUNA

*Flames blaze against the walls, melting the paint and wall-
paper. Smoke funnels through the air so thickly I can't see. I
gasp for air as I roll out of bed and get down on all fours. The
floor is hot against my palms as I crawl in the direction of my
bedroom door.*

*"Mommy!" I cry as I blindly try to find my way out of my
room. "Mommy, help me!"*

*The fire crackles and sweeps across the room, singeing the
floor, the ceiling, everywhere. My eyes burn against the bright-
ness, and my skin feels like melting wax.*

*"Mommy!" I shout and am turning in the opposite direction
when the fire blocks my path.*

So much smoke. I can't breathe.

*No one is coming for me because I'm a bad girl. No one
helps bad girls. My mom's words echo in my head, and I*

realize in horror that it must be true. No one is going to rescue me. The fire is going to kill me.

I fall flat on the floor as smoke circles me. I gasp for air, but with every breath, my lungs feel smaller, like they're shrinking.

"I can't breathe ..." I choke out as my eyelids drift shut.

Pain, so much pain. Just let me die.

Suddenly, I'm lifted from the floor.

"Hang on, Luna. I'm going to get you out of here." The voice is so familiar, so comforting.

I open my eyes as I'm carried away and search through the smoke, trying to see their face, but all I see are smoke and flames.

Everywhere.

My eyes snap open, and I bolt upright in bed, dripping with sweat. It takes me a second to process that my room isn't on fire, that I'm safe.

I flop back down in my bed and stare up at my ceiling. I haven't dreamt about the fire in a while. I hate that it resurfaced. I don't like being reminded of that night almost fourteen years ago when I thought I was going to die until a fireman carried me out of the house. Or, at least that's what my parents tell me. I'm not so sure. Whenever I dream about what happened, it feels like I knew the person who rescued me. I have no clue why my parents would lie about something like that, though.

I try to go back to sleep, but my mind is too wired, and I end up lying in bed awake until the sun rises.

It's fall break, so I don't have school for an entire week. I hate when we get long breaks, because it means staying home with my mom. She won't let me out of the house, and I have no choice but to spend time with her, cooking, cleaning, and listening to her lectures on why I need to be a better person and how disappointed she is that she even has to tell me this, because I should just *know*. Like I'm the freakin' encyclopedia on being a good girl. I'm not, though. At all.

Since she won't let me have my phone, I know I'll lose all communication with my friends. Thankfully, I managed to send them a text before I handed the phone over, so at least they know what's up.

Toward the weekend, she brings out the photos of her sister, Aunt Ashlynn. In most of them, she looks around the same age as I am and resembles a younger version of my mom. She has freckles on her nose like I do, and for some crazy reason, I find comfort in the fact that I share a trait with the rebel of our extended family. Maybe that makes me a freak. That's okay, though. I can be okay with being a freak.

"See these, Luna?" My mom sits down beside me on the sofa and starts flipping through the photo album. "Look at how she's dressed. Look at the people she's hanging out with. Don't they look horrible? Doesn't she look miserable?"

"Sure," I lie and not very well.

If you ask me, Aunt Ashlynn looks pretty damn happy in most of the photos, smiling and laughing with people I assume are her friends. I wonder if she's still happy now or happier even. Will I ever get to that point too? I really, really hope so.

"What happened to her?" I stare at a photo of her on the beach with a group of friends. She's wearing cutoffs and a bikini top, and her eyes are lit up like she's happy. She looks so carefree, like she's saying to hell with her parents and their rules.

My mom slams the album shut. "How would I know? I haven't spoken to her for almost fourteen years."

Always so secretive and evasive, my mother.

"Don't you miss her?" I question. "Don't you want to know if she's okay?"

"No one misses Ashlynn." She rises to her feet and shoves the album back onto the shelf beside the mantle. "I'm going to cook dinner. Go and work on your homework until it's time to set the table."

"But I already did my homework," I tell her.

"Well, do extra credit, then," she snaps then leaves the room.

Clearly I've pushed some buttons. Maybe if I was the good girl she's trying to force me to be, I'd go up to my room, do extra home, and let this drop. I'm not, though. I'm a kleptomaniac, and apparently a wannabe detective, since I steal the album off the shelf to see if I can figure out what's in it that had my mom all worked up. Once I grab it, I take it to my room, and spend the rest of the night pretending to do fake homework while flipping through the album some more.

I've never had a chance to look at it alone. Being by myself with plenty of time to absorb each moment, I get a sense of peace looking at the photos, which leaves me wondering why it unsettled my mom so much. I try to find the answers in the pages, but can't figure it out. And I know I need to put the album back before my mom notices it's not on the shelf, because I know she will—she's got hawk eyes, that one.

Before I do, I remove a photo of my aunt Ashlynn at the beach and hide it under my mattress. As I fall asleep later, I vow to myself that I'll one day get out of this life. That I'll be as happy as Aunt Ashlynn was in the photos.

Yep, that's gonna be me, lying on the beach one day, smiling, and basking in the sunshine.

At least, that's the plan. And it's an awesome plan that can be doable if I just stay out of trouble until I graduate. It sounds simple in theory except for one small problem.

Grey.

He knows a dark secret of mine. A secret that could alter my future plans if he tattles on me. I need to make sure he doesn't. I'm just not quite sure how to do that.

The next day, I attend church with my family then return home and help my dad clean the garage. We don't talk. My father and I rarely do. I used to think it was because he was a man of few words, but when he's around other adults, he can be quite chatty.

The lengthy, dragged-out week gives me plenty of time to overanalyze what's going to happen with Grey when school starts again. What will he say to me about what happened? Maybe I will luck out, and he won't say anything at all.

Please, please let it be the latter.

I think I might have false hope, though, considering he told everyone I asked him to the dance.

By the time Monday rolls around, I'm forced to face the inevitable. I have to go to school and face Grey, and I have to do it while I'm wearing an outfit pre-selected by my mom.

When the sun comes up, she bursts into my room and picks out a pair of tan slacks two sizes too big along with a cardigan that buttons up to the neck. She even searches my bag to make sure I'm not trying to sneak any clothes out with me.

"Remember to come straight home after school," she reminds me as I grab the car keys from the wall hook. "And don't leave the campus until school gets out, even for lunch. I'll be checking your phone to make sure you don't. And I'm going to call the principal to let him know you're not allowed off campus."

I grind my teeth until my jaw aches. *Do not make this worse by arguing. But I want to. So, so badly.*

"You did this to yourself." She stops stirring the pot to yank on my sleeves and unroll them. "I don't even want to think about how you got ahold of clothes like that. I bet it was from one of those friends of yours."

Lately, she has been putting the blame on my friends whenever I do something wrong, like I've recently fallen in with the wrong crowd. But I've been friends with the same people since elementary school, and she knows this. She just doesn't want to accept that her daughter is deciding to rebel on her own.

"It wasn't my friends." I grab a granola bar and a bottle of juice to take with me so I don't have to stick around and eat breakfast with her. "I bought those clothes myself, mom."

"That makes it worse." She crosses her arms and stares me down. "That means you made bad choices on your own. You can't blame that on anyone else."

"I don't," I mutter with a sigh.

"What did you say?" she asks as she reaches into the pocket of her apron.

I force a big old fake smile onto my face. "I said I'm going to be late for school if I don't get going."

"Fine." She withdraws her hand from her pocket, her fingers enclosed around my phone. "I'm only giving this to you so we can keep an eye on you. If it weren't for the tracking app, I wouldn't let you have it."

"Thanks." I snatch the phone from her and make my escape for the door.

Please, please let her be done now.

"Remember who you are, Luna!" she shouts.

I roll my eyes. She has said the same thing to me every day for the last five years. I want to tell her that I don't know who I am, but that I'm definitely not the daughter she wants. Instead I just give her a thumbs up and rush out the door before she can say anything else.

Once I climb into the car, I text Wynter, one of my bestest friends on the planet since second grade. We were the first two members of our group of five friends. It all started with us, a bottle of nail polish, and Wynter coaxing me into rebelling for the day, although it didn't take that much effort to convince me.

"We can use fingernail polish remover before you go home," she said as she painted my nails a bright pink shade.

I was awestruck by the color. It was the first time I'd ever felt pretty in my life.

"This is fun. And it looks so pretty. Like princess-worthy pretty."

"It's totally princess-worthy," she said with a huge grin on her face.

I smiled, but then my happiness faltered. "I just wish my clothes matched."

"One day, they will," she promised.

And she made good on that promise the day I turned seventeen, and she bought me a new wardrobe, which now is nothing but ashes.

May they rest in peace.

Me: Can u bring me some clothes please?

Wynter: OMG! She gave u your phone back!

Me: Yep. But only so she could keep track of me.

Wynter: She's so crazy. And FYI, I was already planning on bringing u some clothes.

Me: Ur the best. I feel so bad that u gave me all those nice clothes and now they're gone. It's such a waste.

Wynter: It's not your fault your parents are craycray.

Me: I know, but I wish they weren't. Their punishments aren't even in the realm of normalcy.

Wynter: Ur telling me. Remember that one time they made you write I Will Not Color On My Walls a thousand times?

Me: That one was pretty bad … I hated that u were there and had to see me do it.

Wynter: I felt so bad for you. And it never made any sense to me. I mean, they made you write it on the wall and then paint over it. I was like, seriously, wth?

Why would u have her write on the wall about not writing on the wall?

Me: I never understood it, either. But I still don't think it's as bad as burning an entire wardrobe. And now she's got that stupid tracking app on my phone. She's so batshit crazy.

Wynter: Don't worry about the app. Ari's on that. Give him a few days, and I'm sure he'll find some kind of way to get around it. Cause he's awesome like that.

I smile for reals in the first time in three days.

Ari has been one of my closest friends since sixth grade after his family moved to Ridgefield. Since his family didn't grow up here, a lot of people treated him like an outsider. My friends and I, being outsiders ourselves, took him under our wing and showed him the inner workings of our middle school.

I actually have four people I consider my best friends. Together, we make up a group of five very different people who somehow work together. Ari is our computer genius who's really into school and getting good grades. Whenever we have a computer crisis, he's there to hack into whatever we need. He once even changed Wynter's math grade from a D to a C so she'd pass Algebra.

Me: Tell him that he's the bestest, bestest.

Wynter: I thought I was the bestest, bestest. :(

Me: No, you're the bestest, bestest, bestest. But don't tell the others.

Wynter: It's our little secret. ;)

Grinning like a dumb ass, I move to set my phone down in the console when I realize I have an unread message. It was sent while my mom had my phone confiscated and it's not from anyone in my contacts since the number is labeled as unknown. Figuring it has to be spam, I swipe it open.

Unknown: Hello

That's it. That's all it says.

"Definitely has to be spam," I mumble.

Then I set the phone on the console and back the car onto the road. The drive to school takes me about ten minutes, and I dread every second, knowing I'm going to have to see Grey when I get there.

I keep imagining all sorts of scenarios of how he outs my secret, ranging from spreading rumors to there being a giant banner hung over the entrance to the school that announces it. That one seems a bit unlikely, but you never know. And I'll admit when I pull into the school parking lot and spot the banner-free entrance, I let out a relieved breath.

One scenario down. Only about a bazillion to go.

Sighing at that though, I park my car. Then I collect my bag, get out, and take a seat on a bench in the campus yard. I put my backpack on my lap, trying to hide my clothes as best as I can but I might as well be wearing a banner that announces I'm a freak. That's okay, though. I can handle this.

I've handled worse.

Still, I try to busy myself from the stares I'm getting, digging in my bag for a stick of gum. As I do so, I come across a few items I stole a couple of weeks ago. Normally, I hide everything under a floorboard in my closet, but Mom knocked on the door while I was emptying my pockets, and I panicked, stuffing them into my bag, you know, because I'm so, so stealthy like that.

Blowing out a frustrated-with-myself exhale, I pull out one of the items. A ceramic statue of a goose? I hate geese. I really do. They're so mean and noisy. So why did I jack this statue of all things? I don't even need it.

Because I have a problem. I know I do. I just don't know how to break it.

"Dude, what's up with the creepy-ass bird?" Beckett, aka Beck, asks as he squints at the figurine in my hand.

Beck is what most people call the preppy, rich kid of our group. They think he's shallow and spoiled because his parents buy him everything. That's just the surface of Beck, though. There's way more going on underneath his nice clothes and good looks. Like a ton more.

"It's a present for my gran's b-day," I lie. And I hate that I do, but what the hell am I supposed to say. I have sticky fingers and like to steal random shit I have no use for?

He slides onto the bench beside me. "I hate to break it to you, Lu, but your present sucks. It'll seriously give your gran nightmares. It's freaking me out now. I bet it comes to life at night and eats peoples' faces off."

"Okay, first off, gross, and second, you know I suck at picking out presents."

Not wanting to talk about the ugly ass bird anymore, I shove it into my bag. Out of sight, out of mind, right? Nope. Not even close. But whatever. At least, I don't have to look at it's ugly face anymore and all that it represents —the ugliness inside me.

I skim the crowd forming in front of our school. "Where's Wynter?"

He slumps back in the seat, his mood deflating. "She didn't come out of her house this morning when I honked the horn, and she hasn't answered any of my texts."

"Are you two still fighting?" I ask, pulling out my phone.

He props his foot up on his knee and rakes his fingers through his messy, blond hair. "We were never fighting. We just had a mild disagreement." When I elevate my brows at him, his lips quirk. "What? It wasn't a fight. We didn't yell at each other."

"Yeah, because she threw her drink in your face then

left your house before you could yell at her. If she had stuck around, you two definitely would've started yelling." I swipe my finger across the screen of my phone.

Me: Where r u?

Wynter: By my locker, waiting for you with some killer clothes.

Me: Awesome. But just an FYI, I'm with Beckett. He seems upset because you blew him off this morning.

Wynter: He totally deserves it. He called me a drama queen and a spoiled brat in front of the entire school, and he didn't even apologize!

I sigh. Wynter is so about the drama. But Wynter and Beckett didn't used to fight. Back in second grade, Beckett used to have a crush on Wynter and would follow her around like a lovesick puppy. Thankfully, he stopped doing that around fourth grade and decided he just wanted to be friends with her.

Me: He just told me to say he was sorry.

"I didn't do anything that I need to say sorry for," Beck says as he reads the message from over my shoulder.

"You called her a spoiled brat. You know she hates that, Beck." I shoo him away.

"But she *is* a drama queen and a spoiled brat. So am I. She should just own it." He bounces his knee up and down, growing frustrated. "She always acts like a princess in front of everyone when she's drunk. I'm not going to just sit there and put up with her shit."

I push to my feet. "I know you're trying to look out for her, but maybe next time, you should just take her aside and talk to her instead of yelling at her in front of everyone."

"Maybe there won't be a next time," he says. "Maybe I'll finally get sick of her shit and stop apologizing for stuff I don't need to apologize for."

"You know you're not going to do that. She may be a pain in the ass, but she's still your friend."

"I guess so. I just wish she was nicer and would quit freaking out over nothing."

"She's nice when she's sober, just like you're more serious when you are." I sling the handle of my bag over my shoulder. "I'm headed inside. You comin'?"

He shakes his head, staring at the parking lot. "I'm waiting for Ari. I'll catch up you with you later."

Waiting for Ari is code for he's avoiding Wynter and will probably have a guy bitch-fest with Ari. Poor Ari. He's too nice, and he won't say anything to Beck, even if he doesn't want to listen to him complain.

I decide to do Ari a solid and send him a text, warning him about Beck's pissy mood so he'll at least have a choice whether he wants to listen.

After I send the message, I wave good-bye to Beck then weave through the crowd and head toward the school. With the morning sunlight beaming down on me and all the layers I'm wearing, I feel my skin dampening. It's late September, but since we live in a fairly dry and sandy place, the temperatures are still in the high seventies.

I miss my shorts and skirts. I miss the fresh air on my long legs, which are going to get super pasty hidden beneath the god-awful pants my mom is going to make me wear for the rest of my existence.

When I finally make it to Wynter's locker, I'm relieved to see her waiting for me.

"Whoa, she must really be mad at you." Her face pinches with disgust at the sight of my outfit, just like everyone else who has seen me.

I'm jealous of the cut-offs, silk kimono, and platforms she's wearing. On top of being a diva, Wynter is really into clothes and completely obsessed with shoes to the point where we've all questioned if we should give her an intervention about her shoe addiction.

She closes her locker and sits down on the floor, opening a bag of chips. "You should've stopped by my house and changed before you came to school."

"I didn't have time." I sink down on the floor beside her and slump back against the locker. "I don't want to hate my mom, but sometimes, I really do. I'm such a bad person."

"You're not a bad person. I hate my parents some-times, too," she says, munching on a chip.

"Yeah, but I really, really hate them sometimes," I mutter. "And I hate geese too, for no reason at all."

She arches a brow at me. "What the heck are you talkin' about, Lu? Geese? Who cares if you hate geese?"

I shrug. "No one, probably. I'm just pointing out that I have a lot of hate inside me."

"Because you hate geese," she states, obviously confused.

And who can blame her? I can be very confusing sometimes.

"Yeah." I shrug again.

"Dude, you're in a mood," she says with a heavy sigh. "Because of your parents. Always you freakin' parents. But you need to get them out of your head, dude. They're psychos, making you burn all those pretty clothes like that. And psycho aren't worth your time."

I can't help but laugh softly. "I'll try to stop thinking about them then."

"Don't try to. Just do it." She offers me some chips, and I grab a handful. "You're already eighteen, for God's sake. They need to realize they can't control you anymore."

Easy for her to say. Wynter's parents are completely the opposite of mine. They pretty much ignore her and let her do anything she wants. Then again, while she pretends her life is fun, I can tell she gets lonely sometimes.

"I've been trying to say something, but sometimes I feel like I'm speaking in a different language. A made up one that's so complex they can't understand it." I look down at my hideous sweater. "And now I'm starting all over again with these clothes." I make a gagging face. "I look like a teddy bear."

She snorts a laugh. "At least you make a cute teddy bear." She pats my head and grins at me when I give her a hardy har look. "And you're not starting over. Your mom can't burn all those parties and fun things we've been doing." She evaluates my outfit again before springing to her feet. "But we do need to get you out of those clothes like ASAP, or I'm going to have to disown you." She smiles so I know she's kidding.

She'd never disown me over clothes and will always be my friend no matter what. Even if she found out about my klepto habit, she'd probably still love me. Still, I'd rather her not know. I'd rather no one knows about that side of me.

But now Grey Sawyer knows, and I'm going to cross paths with him multiple times today. And... Well, I'm not sure what's going to happen, since I've never been in this situation before.

"Are you okay?" Wynter asks as she opens her locker

and picks up a small stack of folded clothes from the top shelf. "You look like you're sick."

"I'm good." I stand up and stretch out my legs. "I'm just ready to get out of this outfit."

She gives me *the look* as she hands me the clothes. The look that lets me know she can see right through my lying bull crap, and it usually leads to her prying.

"You sure? Because you can always talk to me about anything." Her eyes light up as she claps her hands together. "You know what we should do? We should track down Willow and the three of us ditch today. We can have a girls' day out and binge on ice cream. We haven't done that in forever."

That sounds like an awesome idea, but then she'll hold to her word and make me tell her what's bothering me. While I hate keeping stuff from her, confessing my worries with Grey discovering my klepto side means confessing things I'm kind of ashamed of. Hopefully, Grey will keep his mouth shut; otherwise, the rumors will spread through the school like a wildfire.

"I can't ditch today. I have a test in math. Plus, my mom's got the principal on Luna watch." I take the clothes from her and head toward the bathroom. "How about a rain check? Maybe next week sometime?"

"Okay." She keeps giving me *the look* as I wave good-bye then duck into the bathroom.

I peel off the heavy sweater and slacks then put on the

black tank top and plaid shorts Wynter brought me. We don't wear the same size shoes, so I'm stuck wearing my tattered sneakers, but they look okay with the outfit.

I stuff the sweater and jeans into my backpack so I can put them back on after school. Then I pop my head-phones in and crank up a song. School is one of the few places where I can actually listen to music I like. The rhythm soothes me as I head to my first class, even though school doesn't start for another fifteen minutes.

Since it's a little early, I expect the classroom to be empty, but when I walk in, Grey Sawyer is sitting at one of the desks.

Of freakin' course. Because why wouldn't he be?

He's wearing a faded black Henley and a pair of worn jeans, his brown hair scraggly but sexy, looking perfectly put together like he did the other day when he saw who I really am.

I start to back out of the room, trying to be a sneaky ninja, but he looks up at me before I can make my escape. For a split second, his blue eyes widen, but then he gives me that lazy, I'm-the-shit smile. Even after everything that has happened, the look makes my heart go all kinds of crazy in my chest. Because I'm a dumbass like that.

His lips suddenly move as he says something to me.

I tug on the cords of the headphones and pull them out of my ears. "What? I couldn't hear you."

A sparkle of amusement dances in his eyes. "I said, hey, how's it going?"

"Um... Good," I reply, hitching my thumb under the handle of my bag, trying to be all casual like him and I talk every day. But we never do. At all. *This is so weird.* And honestly, I kind of want to bail. But I force myself to stay put and try to pick up on his vibe so I can see where he's standing with this whole klepto secret of mine. "How's stuff going with you?"

"The same. You know, just living life and all that shit." He briefly studies me before he returns to scribbling in his notebook.

That's it? No, "Hey, crazy shoplifting girl"? No, "I saw you the other day stealing from Benny, the nicest old man on the planet"? No, "Here's your jacket back, you dirty little thief"?

I reluctantly sit down at a desk across from him. The room is so quiet I can hear the sound of his pencil scratching across the paper. I retrieve my phone and check my messages to kill time. But the only message I have is another one from that unknown number.

Unknown: How are you?

Clearly, they have the wrong number, so I send a quick text back.

Me: I think you have the wrong number.

Then I check my emails all while hyperaware that Grey is right there. Usually, that alone makes me a little bit nervous, but now my nerves are even more jumbled. I feel exposed and very uncomfortable in my own skin. And I don't like the feeling. At all.

Would he just stop looking at me?

Huh, that's a first.

"Have you talked to Beck this morning?" Grey abruptly asks, startling the living daylights out of me that I almost drop my phone.

I quickly recover, though, and steady my voice. "Yeah, I saw him, like, fifteen minutes ago. Why? Did you need to talk to him or something?"

He shrugs. "I just needed to get something from him but haven't had time to track him down."

"Just send him a text and tell him to bring it to you." I force myself to meet his gaze and point at the window. "Or you can just go outside and search the quad. I'm sure he's still out there." *Bitching Ari's ear off about Wynter.*

"I would, but I can't leave the classroom." When I stare at him in confusion, he looks down at the notebook on his desk, his cheeks reddening with embarrassment. "I'm on academic probation, and I'm trying to get caught up on some assignments so I won't miss Friday's game. And I know if I walk out of here, I'll get caught up with other stuff and won't come back. Being in a classroom ... There are less distractions." He lifts his gaze back to me and shrugs.

He's acting so casual. Maybe he's going to let the stealing thing go.

Or maybe this is just a trick in some sort of plot to take me down.

I roll my eyes at myself. Dude, I've been watching too many spy movies lately.

"Just text Beck, then. I'm sure he'll bring you … whatever you need." But what does he need from Beck?

"I would, but I … I didn't bring my phone." He stares at the trees, avoiding my gaze, seeming less confident than he normally is.

This is so weird. But then again, this whole exchange is weird since the two of us have barely spoken since the dance invite fiasco.

"Another distraction?" I wonder.

He nods, turning his head toward me. For some reason, I feel like he's lying. I don't know why or why it even matters, but I don't understand why someone would lie about not having their phone with them.

"I can text him for you," I offer, hoping that maybe if I'm nice to him it'll get me on his good side.

He exhales audibly. "Thanks, Luna. That'd be awesome."

"It's not that big of a deal," I say as I type Beck a message.

Me: Hey! U need to hit up Mr. Gartying's classroom. Grey's stuck in here and says you're supposed to

bring him something. I'm hoping it's not what I think it is, though, because now I feel like an accomplice. ;)

Beckett: Nope, it's exactly what u think it is. Don't worry, though. I'm sure you look hot in handcuffs.

I roll my eyes. Well, at least he's in a better mood.

Beckett: Tell Grey I'm on my way ... Although, I didn't know u two hung out.

Me: We don't. We're both just stuck in the classroom together.

Beckett: Why r u stuck there?

I consider telling him it's because I'm avoiding Wynter, but that'd give him an open invitation to invite me to his Wynter Bitch Fest and I really don't want to attend.

Me: I needed to get an assignment sheet I lost.

Beckett: Gotcha. Tell Grey I'll be there in a min.

"He says he's on his way," I tell Grey as I set my phone down on the desk. I slant to the side to dig out my book from my bag, figuring that's the end of our conversation. But when I straighten back up, he's staring at me with hesitancy written all over his face.

"Can I ask you a question?" he asks cautiously.

I stiffen. *Oh, great, here it comes. I can almost hear it now. Why are you such a little thief? You evil villain.*

I try to keep the most blasé attitude ever, but probably fail. "Um ... Yeah ... I guess so."

"I don't want you to feel uncomfortable or anything,

but if I don't ask, I'm not going to be able to stop thinking about it." He fiddles with a button on the sleeve of his shirt. "Is everything okay with you?"

My brows knit. "What do you mean?"

"The store the other day ..." He scoops up his bag from the floor and sets it on the desk. "When I saw you stealing"—he unzips the bag, retrieves my jacket, and hands it to me—"I just wanted to make sure you were doing okay."

And there it is, the moment I've been waiting for.

My palms sweat as I take the jacket from him. "I don't ... I didn't mean ... I can't ..."

How am I supposed to explain why I stole some of the stuff that was in the pocket of the jacket? How am I supposed to explain why I steal? I wish I was more like Wynter. If she was in this position, she'd just play it off as being a badass rebel, maybe even flirt with him a little bit, you know give him a flirty smile while batting her eyelashes. But if I even attempted to try that, I'd probably look like some crazed smiling clown that got something in her eye.

"I'm fine ... Thanks ... for helping me," I cringe at how stupid I sound.

"Don't worry about it," Grey says. "I get it."

Um.... What? "Get what?"

He offers me a sympathetic smile that only puzzles

me more. "That sometimes people have to do extreme things to survive."

I'm even more confounded. Does he think I was shoplifting because I have to? Like I need all those things I stole? Is that why he helped me out?

I should correct him, tell him I wasn't surviving anything except the frustrations in my life. I just have issues, and I'm a terrible, messed up person. But before I get the chance, Beck strolls into the classroom. Although, I'm not sure if I would've anyway.

"Aw, look at this. My two favorite people in the whole, wide world hanging out." Beck plants his ass on my desk. "What a great way to start the day."

I note his bloodshot eyes. *"You're high already,"* I mouth with an arch of my brow.

He grins goofily and mouths, *"I needed cheering up."*

I bite back a smile. When Beck's in a good mood, he can be quite charming, but I don't want to encourage him to go into stoner talk mode, which usually leads to him babbling about life's meaning and also how they get so much cheesy flavor into Cheetos.

He winks at me before turning to Grey. "So you're still on academic probation, huh? That sucks."

"Yeah, I'm hoping I'll catch up by the end of the week so I can play in Friday's game," he grumbles in frustration. "But I'm not sure if I'll be able to pull it off. I suck at this class."

Beck deliberates something before his gaze glides to me. "Luna's pretty good. Maybe she can help you."

Wait... What?

"Um... Willow is better than I am." I give him a pleading look not to push this. Even before Grey found out I'm a klepto, I don't think I could've handle being alone with him. "You should ask her to do it."

Beck dismisses me with a wave of his hand. "Don't listen to Luna," he tells Grey. "She's just shy."

"No, I'm not." I blast Beck with a dark look, promising him all sorts of dark things that I'll never really do and we both kind of know that. "I'm being honest. I'm not as good at this class as Willow is, and she's a way better tutor."

"I'd love it if you would, but it's okay if you don't want to," Grey says, but he seems disappointed.

Beck gives me a what's-wrong-with-you look that makes me feel like the biggest jerk ever. I'm being rude after Grey saved my butt from getting busted at Benny's. I kind of owe him.

"No, it's okay," I tell Grey. "If you want me to tutor you, I will." And there's my fake smile that I love so much.

Grey smiles a full-on, genuine smile. "Thanks. I really appreciate it, and I promise I'll be the best student ever."

I return his smile, but on the inside, I'm a wreck. Why the heck did I just agree to tutor him? Grey freakin' Sawyer. The guy who made me feel like a loser. The guy who knows my dirty, little secret. And now I'm just going to, what? Spend hours with him, trying to help him get better with English class, and hope he doesn't want to talk about what I did?

Then there's my mom. She's going to freak if she finds out I'm hanging out with a guy, even if it's just to study. She always gets that way when I try to spend time with guys she doesn't know. She still acts like a weirdo whenever I mention Ari and Beckett.

Maybe I would've retracted my offer. But then the bell rings, and people come pouring into the classroom and that's that.

And while there's a distraction, Beckett pulls a crinkled envelope from his pocket and lays it on Grey's desk.

"Thanks, man." Grey doesn't appear very happy about the envelope as he picks it up and stuffs it into his backpack. Then he collects a small box from his backpack, and with his fingers gripping it tightly, he hands it to Beck. "Here you go."

"Thanks, man," Beckett says, taking the box from him. "And let me know what you decide."

Grey bobs his head up and down, shoving the envelope into his bag.

Okay, what the heck was that about?

I attempt to capture Beck's gaze to see if I can read him, but he refuses to make eye contact with me.

"I should probably bounce. I do have class," Beck says to no one in particular.

Just then, Logan, one of Grey's friends, drops his books on the desk in front of mine. "What's up, dumbass?" he greets Grey and Beckett. Then his gaze lands on me, and a grin plasters across his face. "Hey, what happened to the grandma outfit you were wearing this morning?"

"I ditched it," I say in a clipped tone while opening up my textbook.

I hate Logan with the bane of a thousand suns and I don't even care if that makes me overdramatic.

"Smart move," he tells me with a smirk. "You looked like a hideous beast."

I start to calculate in my head if it'd be worth the trouble I'd get into if I bitch slapped his face.

Maybe...

"Dude, shut up." Beck rises to his feet and gets in Logan's face. "Don't talk to her like that."

"Beck, it's fine." I snag his sleeve and haul him back, not wanting him to get in a fight. "He's right. I did look like a hideous beast."

"See? She agrees with me." Logan flashes me what he probably thinks is a charming grin.

I stare at him, unimpressed.

"I thought I was having flashbacks from last year," Logan rambles on, "when you used to dress like a homeless person. Glad you weren't stupid enough to go back to that look."

"Maybe I was homeless," I tell him. "You don't know."

"Are you?" he questions, seeming way too intrigued by the idea.

Foul words bite on the tip of my tongue, and maybe this time I would've said them, but Beck speaks first.

"Just say the word, and I'll punch him in the face," he says to me, looking eager to please.

I'm not about to get Beck into trouble. Although, the idea of watching Logan get punched in the face does sound mighty appealing.

"Beck, I said it's—"

"Quit being an asshole, Logan," Grey suddenly snaps in a harsh tone. He keeps his gaze fixed on his book, flipping through the pages. "Not everyone has the privilege of being a spoiled, rich kid who never has to worry about money."

Beck gives me a questioning and I shrug, feeling equally as confused.

Beck leans in and puts his lips beside my ear. "Why is Grey Sawyer standing up for you? I love you to death, Lu, and I think you're amazing, but Grey doesn't get involved with other people's drama." He moves back, raising his voice. "That's my thing."

"Yeah, it for sure is." I flash him a cheeky grin. "And maybe you should really think about what you just said, considering you're always chewing out Wynter for being a drama queen."

His brows furrow as if he's just realizing they both share the same trait. "Interesting thought process." He rubs his jawline. "I'm going to have to think about that one for a while."

"Maybe you should do that when you've done a little less …" I put two fingers up to my lips and suck in a breath.

He aims a finger at me as he backs down the aisle. "Good idea. Although, I'll probably forget about this conversation by the time that happens."

"Beckett Vincent, get to class," Mr. Gartying barks as he strides into the classroom, carrying a stack of papers.

"Yes, sir." Beckett salutes the teacher before spinning on his heels and disappearing into the hallway.

Mr. Gartying shakes his head as he sets the papers down on his desk. "Everyone, take a seat and turn to the page written on the board while I take roll."

As I open my book to the correct page, I rack my mind for an excuse to give Grey that will get me out of tutoring him. But everything I come up with seems lame and rude.

"You okay?" Grey whispers to me from across the aisle. "I know Logan can be a dick sometimes."

"Yeah, I'm just peachy," I reply. "He was right about my outfit anyway."

"It doesn't matter if he was right." He keeps his voice low. "He shouldn't be an asshole just because he's rich and doesn't know what it's like to struggle."

My gut twists again as I become aware that he really does think I was stealing because I was poor.

I am a terrible person.

"Grey, I wasn't stealing because of …" I trail off, fearing what everyone will find out if I say it aloud. I'm scared they'll find out I'm not as good of a person as people think. And most of all, I'm afraid of what will happen if word somehow gets back to my parents.

"Don't worry; I won't tell anyone." He pauses, looking as though he's having a mental tug-of-war with himself. "Luna, I'm here if you need to talk. I know you have friends, but I just wanted you to know that." He smiles at me as he sits back in his seat.

"Okay … thanks …"

I feel so lost. Why is he being nice to me? Does he feel sorry for me because he thinks I'm poor? Or is it simply because he's trying to be a nicer person now?

As class begins, I'm left with a handful of unanswered questions that I really need to figure out the answers to.

LUNA

By LUNCHTIME, my brain is drained. I spent half the day obsessing over why Grey was so nice to me and whether he'll keep his promise not to tell anyone. I haven't heard any rumors in the hallways, so that has to be a good sign, right? Or is he playing a game with me? Toying with my emotions so he can get even more sick satisfaction when he tells everyone?

After I grab some snacks and a soda from the vending machines, I join Ari, Beckett, and Wynter outside, under the trees. We sometimes leave campus to eat, but my friends always stick around with me and offer moral support when I have to ride out my mother's punishments.

"This is the worst idea ever." Wynter playfully whacks Beckett in the back of the head as she sits down on the grass beside me, and he blasts her with a nasty look. "Why would you get Luna into this kind of situation? Why, Beck? Why? You know how much she hates Grey Sawyer."

"Hate is a strong word... I don't hate him." I rip open a bag of cheese crackers.

"That's because you're too nice." Wynter steals a cracker from my bag and pops it into her mouth. "But deep down, you kinda, sorta hate him, even if you won't admit it. You have since sophomore year."

"I still don't know if I'd use the word hate," I tell her, but she just rolls her eyes, *like okay, sure you don't.*

I sigh, knowing there's no use arguing with her. There never really is.

"Hey, I never made Grey pay for spreading that rumor about you back in tenth grade, did I?" Beck declares as he slides on his sunglasses. "I should probably do something about that."

"You mean, like manipulating Luna into tutoring him?" Wynter asks, rummaging through her purse. "Because that's a great freakin' way to make him pay. He ends up with good grades, and Luna ends up traumatized from his douche-baggery."

"Hey," I protest. "I'm not going to get traumatized by it. I'm not that weak.

"No one's saying you're weak," Wynter insists. "But

tutoring Grey could be traumatizing for you, considering your guys' history."

"And there's that psych class rearing its ugly head again," Beck mumbles.

Wynter throws a chip at him and it pegs him in the back of his head. But he just scoops it up and pops it into his mouth.

"Yummy," Beck says, grinning at Wynter.

Her lip twitches. "Whatever happens between Luna and Grey is on you."

"Luna didn't have to agree to tutor him," Ari interrupts, picking the crust off his sandwich. "She could've said no if she didn't want to do it."

I raise my head. "Yeah, what he said."

Wynter points a finger at Ari. "Don't be a traitor, Ari. Remember who loves you more."

Ari adjusts his square-frame glasses and brushes his shaggy, brown hair out of his eyes. "Since when do you love me more? Because Beck wasn't the one who yelled at me for spilling his beer at the party the other night."

"Hate to break it to you, dude, but when it comes to loving you more, I think Wynter's the better choice," Beck tells Ari as he scrolls through his phone. "I mean, I'm all for an occasional bromance here and there, but love really isn't my thing."

Ari rolls his eyes. "You know that's not what I meant. I

just meant that most of the time, you're nicer than she is, but now I'm going to take it back."

Wynter grins smugly at Beck. "See. I'm the nicer one."

Beck snorts a laugh. "Yeah, okay."

Wynter lightly smacks Beck's arm, but he ignores her, which seems to irritate her more. She places her hands on her hips and starts teasing him about being a pothead until Beck finally scowls at her. Then she smiles, satisfied with herself.

Ari and I exchange a look. We had a conversation once about the two of them probably secretly being in love, and all the fighting is just sexual tension. That's Ari's theory, anyway. I'm not really buying into it just yet. I wonder if they've known each other for so long they have more of a sibling relationship than anything.

"So, are you really going to tutor Grey Sawyer?" Ari asks me over Beck's and Wynter's bickering.

I waver. "I don't want to, but I already told him I would." I stuff a cracker into my mouth. "And I can't think of an excuse to get out of it without sounding like a jerk."

Ari bites into his sandwich. "You're allowed to be a jerk every once in a while. You don't have to be so nice all the time."

"I could say the same thing to you," I quip cheekily. "And besides, I'm not nice all the time. You, however, might be the nicest guy to ever exist."

"Hey, I can be mean sometimes," Ari tries to argue, peeling more crust off his bread.

I laugh so hard a pig snort. "You *so* cannot. You're, like, the nicest guy ever."

"No way," he insists, but he's grinning. "Everyone can be mean sometimes."

"Okay, but still—"

"God, I'm so tired I can't even see straight." Willow drops her bag next to me then dramatically falls down on the grass and drapes her arm over her head.

"Napping is a great cure for that," Beck says, stealing the bottle of water from Wynter's hand. "Trust me. I'm an expert."

"I'm sure you are, but I can't take a nap right now." Willow unties the over-shirt that's around her waist, balls it up, and tucks it under her head like a pillow. "My mind won't slow down."

"I have something that can help with that," Beck offers, reaching for his bag.

I know what's gonna take out too.

"No way." I point a finger at Beck. "I'm not going to let you corrupt Willow."

"I'm just giving her a choice." Beck raises his hands in front of him, surrendering. "Chillax, Lu."

"He's not going to corrupt me," Willow murmurs, her eyelids drifting shut. "I'm already corrupted."

The four of us look at each other then burst into a fit of laughter.

Willow contains a smile. "Mock all you want, but I've done some really bad things. I've even come this close"—she holds up her finger and thumb an inch apart—"to being a bad girl."

"Sticking your gum on the bottom of a desk doesn't count," Beck says, resting his arms on his knees. "Admit it, Wills, you're too sweet to be bad."

"Yeah, you're probably right." She smirks a little as she rolls on her side and cranes her neck to look at him. "That's more Wynter's and your thing. Ari, Luna, and I have to be good to make up for all the bad stuff you two do."

"Oh, you think I'm bad, huh?" Beckett teases as he jumps to his feet. "I'll show you how bad I can be."

Willow's eyes pop open, and she scrambles to get up, but Beck snags her by the back of her shirt, yanks her back against him, and tickles the crap out of her.

"Beck, stop!" Willow begs as she tries to squirm out of his hold. "I take it back. You're good!"

"Say I'm a good boy." Beck tickles her sides. "And that you love me."

"Fine! You're a good boy, and I love you!" she manages to get out through her laughter.

Instead of letting her go, he lies on the ground and brings her with him. Then he rolls on his side and tucks his arm underneath her head. With how close they act, I sometimes wonder if there's something going on between the two of them. If there is, though, no one seems to know about it. And I'm not going to pry the details out of them.

We all have our secrets.

"My arm's a better pillow for napping," Beck insists as he presses his chest against Willow's back.

"No way," Willow says, but she rests her head on his arm, and seconds later, her eyelids lower.

Beck looks proud of himself for getting her to relax. It's a hard thing to do with Willow since she's usually stressed out. She's been since the day we became friends back in third grade. She was the quiet, shy girl who wore old clothes that were a little too big for her. She always spent recess on the swings by herself until the day Wynter announced, "She seems sad. We should make her come play hopscotch." So we marched over there and made her play with us. She didn't seem too reluctant, though. In fact, she seemed grateful someone had made the effort to get to know her.

But Willow has every reason to be stressed. On top of helping her parents out financially by working almost every weekend, she's also trying to get an academic scholarship and spends crazy amounts of hours doing schoolwork.

Beck reaches over with his free hand and steals a

handful of crackers from the bag on my lap. "Eat before you sleep," he says to Willow, offering her the crackers. "You're too skinny."

Willow opens her eyes and takes the crackers from Beckett. "Thanks, Beck. I don't know what I'd do without you."

"Probably laugh less." He gently pinches her in the side before nuzzling against her.

"That's not fair," Wynter says to Beck with her lip jutted out. "You're always nice to Willow and Luna, but all you ever do for me is call me a spoiled brat."

"That's because Will and Lu don't call me a rich douche," Beckett mutters. "Nice people get treated nicely."

I internally grimace. What is with all the nice comments getting thrown in my direction today? All this nice talk is starting to give me a stomachache.

"Okay, I kind of see your point," Wynter muses thoughtfully, but then her mood fizzles as her gaze darts toward the school. "Oh, boy. Here comes drama."

I track her gaze to see Grey heading in our direction. That lazy smile spreads across his face when he notices me looking at him, and my heart betrays me by fluttering in my chest like a lunatic.

"What a cocky asshole, just like every other damn jock in this school," Wynter mutters, glaring at him. "He sees some girls looking in his direction and automatically thinks we're checking him out."

She might be wrong, considering I was just kinda, sorta ogling him. But again, lemme stress, we all have our secrets.

"Hey, I'm a jock," Beck protests. "And I don't think that."

"You're not a jock," Wynter insists. "You just play sports."

Beck tips his head, slides his sunglasses down, and looks at Wynter. "What's the difference?"

"Jocks are sports guys who hang out with other sports guys and obsess about sports and think they're so awesome because they can throw and kick a ball," Wynter explains. "You hang out with a bunch of weirdoes who don't ever want to talk about sports. See? That's how much we love you, enough that we haven't let you fall into the jock mold."

"Gee, thanks," Beck says dryly.

"You're welcome," Wynter singsongs, beaming. "And you say I never compliment you."

Le sigh. Here they go again.

I give Ari a look and he starts to return it when his expression fumbles, his gaze straying to something over my shoulder.

I start to turn to see what in the crazy daisies has got

him looking as confused as watching Logan try to solve a math equation when I hear Grey say, "Hey."

Ari, Wynter, Beck, and I all look up at him, while Willow remains lying on Beck's arm with her eyes closed. Some of Grey's confidence diminishes from our scrutinizing gazes.

"Are you lost or something?" Wynter points at the school. "The gym's that way."

"I know where the gym is." Grey shoots me a quizzical glance, like what's your friend's deal.

I just shrug, wanting to take Wynter's side, but Grey also knows my dark secret...

I gotta be Switzerland on this one.

Wynter crisscrosses her legs then rests back on her hands. "So why aren't you there?" she asks Grey. "That is where all you jockheads hang out all the time, right?"

"Be nice," I give Wynter a pressing look.

"Why? He and his steroid friends aren't nice to anyone other than Dixie, Mixie, and the ditz squad." Wynter looks at Grey with her brows raised, challenging him to argue with her.

Grey seems the slightest bit amused, the corners of his lips twitching. "If you're talking about the girls on the cheerleading squad, then I think their names are Dixie and Pixie, not Dixie and Mixie."

"You'd know better than I would"—Wynter folds her arms across her chest and pins him with her best sassy smirk—"since you've probably screwed every single one of them."

Ari chokes on a mouthful of food while Beck grumbles, and Willow bites down on her bottom lip to restrain a smile while keeping her eyes closed.

Grey lifts a shoulder. "I guess you'd know better than I do since you seem to know everything about me."

Okay, time to interrupt before Wynter gives Grey incentive to out that I have klepto tendencies.

"You said you needed to talk to me?" I say to Grey, leaping to my feet.

His gaze sweeps across my friends then lands back on me. "Can we talk somewhere more private?"

Wynter mouths, *"Privately? No way."*

I turn my back on Wynter and nod. "Yeah, sure."

"Be careful, Lu!" Wynter hollers as Grey and I start across the grass toward the center of the quad. "Remember tenth grade."

My cheeks flood with heat. I love Wynter to death, but she really needs to stop saying every single thing that pops into her head.

Grey remains silent as we make our way around the people eating lunch on the grass. I catch people gawking at us and cringe when we pass by Piper Talperson, Grey's girlfriend for the last year.

Grey has stuck to his type over the years, and Piper fits it impeccably: a popular cheerleader with curves. Her hair and makeup are always flawlessly done, and she wears the latest fashions. Honestly, she reminds me a lot of Wynter. Only, Wynter has more of an edge to her style and is a hell of a lot nicer.

Looking annoyed, Piper stands up from the bench she's sitting on and pushes her way over to us.

"Babe, where are you going?" she asks Grey, snagging the sleeve of his shirt.

Grey stops, casting an uneasy glance at me before facing her. "I just need to talk to Luna about something for class," he explains.

"Oh, hey, is it Luna?" she says like she just noticed me standing there and has never met me before.

"Yeah." I force a smile, but dude, is this one tougher to put on then the rest of the ones I've worn today.

Piper is a... Well, the nicest way I can put it is that she's not a very nice person. I've seen her do a lot of cruel things, like openly mocking the other girls in our gym class, calling them fat and ugly and flat chested—yeah, the last one was directed toward me. She also loves to gossip and has destroyed many people's reputations by outing their secrets.

Her lip curls at me before she zeroes in on Grey again. "I thought we were going out to lunch together." She tucks a strand of her long, brown hair behind her ear and flutters her eyelashes as she peers up at him.

"I told you I couldn't today," Grey says, sounding tired.

She juts out her bottom lip. "But you've been saying that every day. I'm getting bored of staying at school for lunch."

"Then leave campus with your friends." Grey slips his arm from her hold. "You'd be happier if you went with them, anyway."

"Why are you being such a dick?" She glares at me like it's somehow my fault.

Not wanting to get involved in their drama, I resist an eye roll and tell Grey, "I'm going to go wait over there."

Grey nods, seeming relieved. "Yeah, okay."

I take shelter in the shade and mess around with my phone while casting glances in their direction. At first, they seem like they're having a heated argument, but then Grey gives her a kiss and walks away with a smile on his face.

I find myself wondering what it would be like to have a boyfriend. I've never had the opportunity to date anyone I've liked. I've never even kissed a guy—well, unless you count the time Ari, Wynter, Willow, Beck, and I played spin the bottle and I had to kiss Beck. It was painfully awkward to say the least, and the two of us couldn't even look each other in the eye for a month. After that, I put a ban on playing any more kissing games with the four of them—

My phone buzzes with an incoming text.

Unknown: Nope, I'm pretty sure I don't have the wrong number.

Dude, what is this person's deal? They clearly have the wrong number since I haven't given my number out to anyone recently.

I'm about to text them back just that when Grey walks up to me.

"Sorry about that," he apologizes.

"No worries." I put my phone away and follow him as he rounds the side of the school and back to where no one hangs out. It's also where Piper and the rest of Grey's friends can't see us.

He doesn't say anything right away, only stares at the parking lot where the teachers usually park. I spot Ms. Belingfutor, my Biology teacher, taking a smoke break out by one of the cars, and for some reason, that makes me giggle.

"What's so funny?" Grey asks with a somewhat intrigued, somewhat confused smile.

"It's nothing." I point over at Ms. Belingfutor puffing away. "I just think it's funny seeing teachers do stuff like that. It makes them seem normal, which just seems weird."

Grey glances from Ms. Belingfutor to me. "I get what you're saying. There was one time I caught Coach feeling up his wife in his office. But that was a little less funny and a lot more disturbing than watching Ms. B smoke."

I snort a laugh. "Are you serious?"

He nods with his eyes wide, as if he's reliving the horror. "It was horrible and so embarrassing, but what's even worse was Coach wanted to talk about it and make sure I wasn't traumatized. And I was, but I'd never tell him that." He folds his arms across his chest and shifts his weight as his forehead creases. "I've never told anyone that story. If the guys on the team ever found out, they'd never let me live it down."

My laughter fizzles a bit as I assess him. "Then why did you tell me?"

"I don't know … maybe because you're not on the team, and you're not a guy, so I know you won't ask stupid questions, like if Coach's wife is hot."

I get his point, but still, it's not like we're even close to being friends, which brings up the huge question: why are we here?

"You said you wanted to talk to me about something, and I'm guessing it's not about how hot your coach's wife is."

"Yeah." He massages the back of his neck tensely. "I wanted to talk to you about this whole tutoring thing. I just didn't want to do it in front of your friends. They're kind of intimidating."

"*My* friends are intimidating?" I almost laugh. "Your friends are always making fun of people."

"That's not what I meant," he says in a panic. "I just meant they really care about you. And I knew that if I had this conversation in front of them, it'd be analyzed later and that can be ..."

"Intimidating," I finish.

He bobs his head up and down, stepping closer to me, and I have to tip my chin up to look at him.

"Any outsider who approaches you guys probably feels a little freaked out." A lopsided smile tugs at his lips, and I stare at his mouth a few seconds too long, you know, just living up to my freak reputation.

"People think that about you, too. You can be intimidating to approach, especially when you're with your friends. Trust me, I know." I want to smack myself in the head for subtly mentioning the tenth grade dance. "You know what? Forget I said that."

"No, it's okay." He cracks his knuckles, averting his gaze to the ground as he mutters, "I get where you're coming from. Back then ... I was an asshole."

A beat of silence goes by.

Can things get anymore awkward?

I clear my throat a few times. "You said you wanted to talk about the tutoring thing."

A relieved breath puffs from his lips. "I just wanted to see where you want to meet up and what time."

"The only place I'm allowed to go other than my house is the library, and I don't want to meet up at my house." When his forehead creases, I add, "Trust me; you don't want to go there, either."

"Okay." He waits for me to embellish, but I'm not about to give him the details about my insane home life. "So I guess it's the library."

"Sounds good. You want to meet around four?"

He scratches the back of his neck. "I have practice after school. Maybe around six?"

"Sure. That works." As long as my mom isn't on one of her lock-me-in-my-room-after-dinner kicks.

"Okay, it's a date." One side of his mouth pulls into that sexy half-grin I've seen him use on a ton of girls over the years.

I smile back, but I'm totally confused. *Date?* Why did he call this a date?

He didn't mean it literally. He has a girlfriend, for God's sake. Jesus, Luna, stop being such a dumbass.

"Thanks for doing this," he adds. "It's really awesome of you. Most people aren't that nice."

I'm not that nice! Why does everyone think this?

I force a tight smile. "It's not a big deal. Besides, Beck would freak if I didn't help you, and then you didn't get to play in Friday's game. He hates losing."

"I think everyone does … except maybe you. You seem too sweet to get upset about something like that."

I resist a sigh. "Tell that to Wynter. She won't play board games with me anymore."

"So, you're a sore loser?" He pokes me in the side teasingly, and I flinch from the sudden unexpectedness of the touch.

Not that it's bad. It's just... weird.

"Um, yeah." I struggle to remember what we are talking about as I grow flustered. *Board games. Sore losers.* "Once, I threw all the cards out her bedroom window when we were playing Texas Hold'em, and I lost, like, ten hands in a row. Then there was the whole Candyland fiasco."

"What happened with that?" he asks, seeming strangely intrigued by my board game dark side.

"I broke the heads off all the pieces." I try not to smile, even though it's kind of funny now. "But keep in mind that I was only eight, and I don't have any brothers or sisters. Whenever I played games at home, I played by myself and always won."

He struggles not to laugh. "Wow … that's…"

"Ridiculous?" I offer. "Insane? Neurotic?"

His grin slips through. "I was actually going to say funny."

"I'm glad you think so, but Wynter didn't. That's pretty much when she stopped playing board games with me. She gave me a chance a few years later, but that ended quickly. I haven't played games since."

He chuckles. "She sounds like a wimp if you ask me. So what if you broke a few game pieces and threw some cards out the window?" He pokes me in the side again, and this time, instead of flinching, my stomach does a kick flip. "I'd play with you."

"Yeah, right. You say that now, but you'd change your mind once you witnessed the nastiness in all its temper-tantrum glory."

He drums his fingers against the side of his legs with his forehead creased. "I'll tell you what. At the end of every tutoring session, how about we play a game of cards?"

"You want to play cards with me after I help you study?" I question with skepticism.

"You say that like it's weird."

It is. And suspicious. "It is weird … You don't seem like the game playing type."

"I love playing cards. I used to play them with my dad." His face pales at the mention of his dad.

I feel horrible that we got on the topic of parents, especially his dad. From what I've heard around school, his dad passed away a few months ago at the beginning of the summer. I'm not sure how, though.

"But, yeah, anyway." Grey clears his throat and glances down at his watch. "I have to meet up with someone. Can you give me your number, just in case something happens and I can't make it tonight?"

I nod and rattle off my number, and he writes it down on his hand with a pen.

When he notes me staring confusedly at the ink on his palm, he explains, "Some friends of mine thought it'd be funny to play catch with my phone, and then one of them accidentally threw it against the wall." He shoves the pen into his back pocket. "See you later tonight." He steps by me to leave, but then stops. "You're okay with getting to the library, right? Because I can come pick you up. I know how super pricey gas is."

I catch the faintest hint of pity in his tone. I should confess right then and there that I'm not poor, that I have my parents' nearly brand new car to drive to the library. Instead, I only mumble, "I'm fine, but thanks for the offer."

"Okay, but if you change your mind, let Beck know. He knows how to get ahold of me." He stands there for a moment longer before hurrying off toward the front of the school.

Why would Beck know how to get ahold of him? The two of them have never been close or anything, and now Beck's suddenly the one who knows how to get ahold of him and is giving him envelopes before class?

For reals, what is going on?

By the time I make it back to my friends, Willow and Wynter have taken off, and Ari is collecting his things to head inside the school. Beck, however, is still sprawled across the grass, looking like he has every intention of staying there forever.

"Beck, can I talk to you for a sec?" I ask as I pick up my bag and the half-eaten bag of crackers off the grass.

He sits up, stretching out his arms. "Sure. What's up?"

"See you guys later," Ari says as he gathers the last of his books. "And, Lu, give me a shout later. I think I might have a solution to your tracking problem."

"Already?" I ask, and he nods. "Thanks, Ari. I don't know what I'd do without you."

"Probably be stalked by your mom a lot more." He glances at the school as the bell echoes through the air. "I should get to class, but text me around seven or eight."

I wave good-bye to him before he turns on his heels and gets swept up in the crowd rushing for the entrance doors.

"Man, your mom's doing that crazy tracking thing again?" Beck gripes as he reaches for his backpack propped against a nearby tree. "What was it about this time?"

"My choice in clothes," I say with a sigh.

"She has control issues."

So do I, Beck. So do I.

But all I say is, "Yeah, she does."

He yawns. "So, what did you want to talk to me about?" He holds up his hands in front of him, his eyes sparkling mischievously. "No, wait, let me guess. You

want to start dating me so you can bring a bad boy home
and drive your mother crazy."

"I thought Willow said you were a good boy," I tease.
"Or is that just when you're around her?"

"I'm whoever I need be at the given moment," he
quips, flashing me his pearly whites. "And right now, I
think you need a bad boy."

"Speaking of bad boys, what was up with that envelope you gave Grey this morning? There weren't"—I look
around at all the people nearby then scoot closer to him
and lower my voice—"drugs in there, were there?"

"Luna, you've known me forever. Do really think I'd
deal drugs in school?"

I shrug. "I don't want to think you'd deal drugs, but
I've seen you give people stuff."

"I never charge for the stuff, though, so it's technically
not dealing. I just share with those who want to partake,"
he says with a devious grin. "And to answer your question about Grey, no, there weren't drugs in that envelope,
but that's all I can tell you."

"How come?" I question.

"Because it's not my place to tell." Beck squints against
the sunlight as he studies me. "What I really want to
know is why you two are suddenly spending time
together. I thought you hated him."

"No, Wynter said I did. I, however, said that hate's a
strong word. I don't think I've ever hated him." And, if

I'm honest with myself, I still have a crush on him after all these years, even after what he did to me. "I've just never talked to him because of that dance thing."

He reaches up to pat my arm. "It's okay not to like everyone."

"I know. But I don't think I should not like Grey unless you know of a reason I shouldn't." It's a lame attempt to get him to confess what was in the envelope. I don't even know why I care so much. Maybe it's because Grey knows stuff about me. Or maybe it's because I'm turning into a nosey person. Who the crap knows.

"Sorry, but I'm not telling you what was in that envelope." He stands up, picking up his backpack from the ground. "But you should probably be careful around Grey. He's an okay guy and everything, but you're too good for him."

"I'm just tutoring him," I remind him as we start toward the school. "And you're the one who got me into that mess.

"Yeah, I really shouldn't talk to people when I'm high. I become this weird, all about the love kind of guy," he says with an innocent shrug. "But I think you'll be okay. Just don't date him, especially when he never apologized for what he did to you."

"This isn't a date. We're meeting at the library, and he has a girlfriend."

"Oh, you can have a date at the library. I dated this girl

once whose mom would only let her go to the library with me because she thought we couldn't do anything there but study. We did a lot of naughty things in the aisle with encyclopedias. There was this one time—"

I throw my hands over my ears. "Gah! I never, ever want to hear about your sex life, Beck. *Ever.*"

Beck laughs but drops the subject.

We walk to school, chatting about the party he's having this weekend and how I need to find a way to get there no matter what because he needs me to DJ for him.

"Beck, I'm not a DJ," I say. "I don't know why you keep insisting I am."

"I know you're not technically a DJ, but you're really good at putting mixes together and running the stereo." He winks at me. "No one else can rock it like you."

"I'll try to make it, but I can't make any promises." I'm already on thin ice as it is.

Still, I find myself feeling hitting a low that I probably won't be able to go. Again, I'll be the one missing out on all the fun. Even with the tracking app off my phone, my parents will never allow me out of the house that late at night, which leaves sneaking out as the only option.

As we reach the entrance of the school, Beck holds the door open.

"Why thank you, sir." I laugh as I step into the hallway.

As my phone vibrates from inside my pocket, I fish it out.

Mom: You are to come straight home after school.

Sighing, I type a reply.

Me: I was already planning on it.

Mom: I know, but sometimes you dilly-dally around with those friends of yours. You better walk through the front door within 15 minutes after school gets out and not a minute later. I know how long it takes to make the drive home. I even clocked it myself today just to make sure.

I shake my head. She really is insane.

Me: Okay, I get it. I'll be there at 3:45.

Mom: I'm serious about this, Luna. You, me, and your father have a lot of talking to do about what I found in your floorboard this morning.

I almost drop the phone. They found my secret hiding place. Oh. My. God. I feel sick. All the things I've hidden in there, things I can't explain how I got, things I'm not supposed to have, like makeup and nail polish and a pair of lacy panties that I've never worn, but she's going to think I did.

"No, God. No, no, no."

"What's wrong?" Beckett asks from right behind me.

"I … um …" I'm too speechless to form words.

Another text buzzes through.

Mom: You're lucky I didn't come and pick you up from school already, but I don't want you to get behind on your schoolwork. Just know that there will be

severe punishments, young lady. I'm not going to let you fall into the darkness. You won't become that girl.

"Tell me what's wrong." Beck lowers his head to level our gazes. "You look like you're about to throw up."

"I think I am." I fold my arm around my stomach. "I-I have to get to class." I run down the hallway before he presses me for answers.

I don't go right to class, though. Instead, I run into the bathroom, lock myself in the stale, and reread the messages, trying to figure out how she found my hiding spot.

She had to be snooping around in my room, but why?

As another messages buzzes through, I wonder if I might have my answer.

Unknown: Secret one revealed. Do I have your attention now?

GREY

"IT SUCKS Coach isn't letting you practice with us," Logan says as I collect my books from the locker. "By the time you get your grades up, you're going to be useless."

"Gee, thanks." I slam my locker shut then rest my shoulder against it. "You don't have to act like an asshole all the time."

He grins arrogantly. "I run this damn school. I can do whatever I want."

"Wow, what a fucking accomplishment. You know there's, like, maybe a hundred people who go to our school, right?"

Logan doesn't bother to move out of the way as a girl tries to squeeze around him to get to her locker.

"God, you've been such a fucking downer lately. What

the hell is wrong with you? Is Piper not putting out or something?"

I push him out of the way to help out the girl, and he stumbles back, his shoes scuffing against the linoleum floor. The girl offers me a tense but grateful smile then quickly spins the combo to her locker.

Logan gives me a dirty look as he regains his footing. "Screw you, man. You think you're better than everyone, but you're not." He backs down the hallway, sneering. "Oh, yeah, and have fun with your little tutoring thing while the rest of us who aren't stupid work our asses off to hold up the team. I'm sure you'll have a blast *trying* to learn shit from *Luna Harvey*." He says her name like there's something funny about it, probably because in tenth grade, he told everyone how she asked me out, and I rudely turned her down because I was a dick back then.

She was shier than she is now, and she wore clothes that covered up every inch of her body. The outfits were always weird, too. Like this one time, she wore a baggy sweater with bright yellow bears on it and a pair of baggy, tan pants that looked big enough to fit a guy. I want to say it didn't matter to me, but I was a jerk. I cared way too much about what people like Logan thought of me. I didn't understand that not everyone had enough money to buy whatever they wanted, including nice clothes. Now I understand more than I want to.

I understand a lot of things now, like when I saw Luna

stealing stuff at Benny's store. All those horrible outfits she used to wear were probably because she couldn't afford anything nicer. She does dress better now, but I've seen her friends giving her clothes during school. It's why I took her jacket. I didn't want her getting into trouble like I did.

I stuff my books in the bag then back down the hallway in the opposite direction as Logan, calling out, "Well, at least I won't be wasting my time by hanging around at the meet up tonight for the millionth time, getting trashed and waiting around for something exciting to happen that never does."

He flips me the middle finger. "Yeah, I'll make sure to tell Piper and Jane that. Guess I'll just have to entertain them both since your dumbass isn't going to be there." He thrusts his hips a few times before spinning around and heading off toward the gym. As he walks under the banner advertising the fall formal in a few weeks, he jumps up, slaps his hand against it, and knocks it down.

He's such an asshole. I don't even know why I'm friends with him anymore other than I've been friends with him forever, and he's just around all the time. I wish I had the balls to end our friendship. I honestly want to with most of my friends, but I'm not sure I could handle being alone. Although, I feel alone even when I'm surrounded by people.

Bottling down my irritation, I shove out the doors

that lead to the side of the school, ready to get the hell away from this place and everyone in it. But Piper cuts me off.

"Hey, baby," she says, walking across the grass toward me. "I'm glad I caught you before you left."

I'm not. "What do you want?"

"God, what's with the attitude?" she snaps. "You've been acting like this for months. It's getting ridiculous."

I take a deep breath and try again, reminding myself that I'm trying to be a better person, and this is not the way to do that. "What's up?"

She arches her back, pressing her chest against mine. "See? There's the old Grey I know and love." Her fingers thread through my hair as she pulls me in for a quick kiss.

My jaw ticks. While I want to appear like I still have my life in control, I don't want to be who I used to be anymore. I want to be someone different, someone nicer. I want to be someone who doesn't lie to their father while he's on his deathbed.

Piper starts yammering about the dance coming up next month, and I zone out, thinking about what my dad said to me right before he died.

"Make sure to live your life to the fullest. Do what makes you happy, Grey." His eyes begged me to understand his full meaning as he clutched my hand. "Surround yourself with people who make you happy. I want you to always be able to look back on your life and smile at all the great things you did."

"And my dress looks so hot." Piper hooks her arms around the back of my neck. "You're going to seriously lose your mind when you see me in it."

I feel like I'm banging my head against a wall. I haven't asked her to the dance yet, and I don't plan on it. Dances are expensive and overrated. Besides, I'm not sure we will still be together in a month. The only reason our relationship has lasted this long is because I went MIA for the entire summer after my father passed away and barely spoke to her or any of my other friends, for that matter. She didn't care that much—no one did—and when we did speak, she complained that I was, as she put it, too depressing to be around.

School has been going for a few weeks now, and she keeps making comments about how different I am. I hate that she doesn't understand. I tried to open up to her about it once, but again, she told me I was being too depressing and quickly shut down the conversation.

She doesn't make me happy.

Why am I still with her?

"Sound good?" Piper asks, batting her eyelashes.

"Um … I guess so," I say, unsure what I'm agreeing to.

She stands on her tiptoes and presses her lips to mine, giving me a deep kiss. "Yummy." She moves back. "Oh, and Grey? No more taking girls around to the back of the school. You're going to upset me. And you know, when I get upset, someone has to pay for it," she says sweetly, but her eyes carry a threat.

I frown as she waggles her fingers at me then ambles back across the grass, swaying her hips.

God, I really need to break up with her, stop dragging out the inevitable. I just don't know how to do it without pissing her off. Piper is all about the drama. I've seen her make it her mission to break down people she doesn't like. She finds out their secrets and tells every person she knows. I don't want to deal with that shit. I just want a quiet, normal life, a fresh start. A second chance to do things better, I guess.

I leave the school, feeling frustrated. As I'm rounding the corner of the building, I hear the sound of fabric ripping. The next thing I know, my books are scattered all over the ground.

Cursing, I slip off the backpack and look at the damage. It tore right along the seam, so I think it's fixable. Still, getting home today is going to be a pain in the ass.

I bend over, pick up my books, and finish the walk around to the back of the school. I move past the cars and the shed woodshop takes place in, hiking all the way to the hill about a half a mile away from school. Then I duck into the trees and retrieve my rusty, piece of shit bike I hid this morning where no one could stumble across it or see me riding it to school.

I hate the bike more than I hate Logan. It represents how much my life has changed over the last few months—falling apart and barely able to hold up my weight. I wouldn't even ride the damn thing except it takes about twenty extra minutes on foot to get home, and that would make me late to therapy/support/whatever you want to call it group. The only other option is to ride the bus, which is never going to happen. I could catch a ride with one of my friends, but they all have soccer practice right now. Besides, that might lead to questions they wouldn't want to hear the answers to. So for now, I'll keep my secrets and just live in a world of lies.

GREY

I MAKE it home with time to spare, dripping in sweat.

"Grey, come play basketball with me!" my eleven-year-old sister Mia shouts as I pedal up the driveway.

"I wish I could, but I have to go somewhere," I say as I jump off the bike and wheel it up to the garage.

She frowns as she dribbles the ball. "You're always too busy."

"I know. I'm sorry." I prop the bike against the garage, feeling bad that I've been such a terrible brother lately. I've just been too busy trying to keep what's left of the family together. "How about I set a couple of hours aside this Saturday? We can do anything you want."

Her eyes glint with hope. "Even if it's going out for ice cream?"

"If that's what you want to do." I just hope I can scrounge up enough change for it.

She frowns again. "But we can't afford stuff like that anymore."

"You shouldn't worry about money, Mia. You're just a kid."

"Everyone else is always worried," she mutters. "I even heard Mom talking to Aunt May about how we're going to end up on the streets. Is that true? Are we going to be homeless?"

Seeing her worry like this breaks my heart.

"No, we're not going to end up homeless," I say, though sometimes I worry about that myself. "Mom just says things sometimes when she gets stressed."

"But we're poor. And don't people who are poor end up homeless?"

"Just because we don't have as much money as we used to, it doesn't mean we're going to be homeless." I take the ball from her and shoot a one-handed basket. "Now start making a list of all the things you want to do on Saturday, and we'll make sure to do as much as we can." That gets her to smile.

"Okay, but it's going to be super long with lots of crazy stuff," she warns as I jog up the stairs. "So be prepared."

"I'll make sure to be ready for all sorts of crazy stuff," I promise her then open the door and step into the kitchen.

On the outside, the house still resembles the same home I grew up in: two stories with trees in the yard and a lawn I'm forced to mow. But that's all just a lie. A façade. On the inside, it's empty.

After my dad passed away four months ago from cancer, my mom has been selling off furniture, appliances we don't need—pretty much anything she can until the house sells.

"We can't afford it anymore," she said to me the day a realtor showed up with a for sale sign.

"But this is Dad's house," I snapped, angry that she was getting rid of the place that carried so many memories of him.

Tears welled in her eyes, and I instantly felt like the worst son in existence. "I know it is," she whispered, "but, Grey, there's not much else I can do. Your father and I … We didn't plan for him to get sick and …" Tears streamed from her eyes as she stared at a framed picture of him on the wall. "I don't know what else to do," she said more to herself.

I dropped the subject after that, even though it kills me every time the realtor shows someone our house.

"You look tired," my mom notes as she glances up from the stack of overdue bills on the kitchen table in front of her.

She's the one who looks worn out with her bloodshot eyes, and she's still wearing her pajamas. She used to be one of those moms who was always up and running before everyone else. Now she's usually late for everything and doesn't have time to clean up. But with everything she's taken on, it's not her fault, and she's still a good mom.

"I stayed up late, trying to catch up on assignments." I set my torn backpack on the table covered with overdue bills. "Can you fix this?"

She picks it up and turns it over, examining the hole in the bottom. "I think I can. What happened? Did you snag it on something?"

"No, it's just old. I knew it was going to happen sooner or later." I open the fridge and hold back a sigh at the lack of food inside.

"Honey, I'm so sorry," she says. "I can buy you a new one if you want me to. I just got some extra shifts at the diner and—"

"Mom, stop worrying. It's not that big of a deal. It's just a backpack." I open the cupboard and grab three packs of fruit snacks. My mom has been bad about stocking the cupboards with food, partly because she's distracted and partly because we're low on cash. "I have to go to that thing again, but when I get back, can you drive me to Benny's? He said to stop by today and fill out an application." I begged him to let me apply because no one else in town would even consider hiring me after the shoplifting ordeal.

She presses her lips together, on the verge of crying. "I hate that they're making you go to these sessions. It's not fair after what you've been through."

"We've all been through stuff," I tell her. "I made the choice to do what I did. I'm just lucky the store owner didn't press charges. And I only have to go for another week. I can make it through one more week."

She nods, dazing off, thinking about God knows what. It could be the bills, her nightshift at the diner she started working at after my dad died, her day job at the pharmacy, or her son who decided to steal a soda, a bag of chips, and a frozen package of steaks and got caught.

The owner agreed not to press charges, just as long as I attended this support group/therapy session. Since I live in such a small town, there aren't any individual sessions, so I have to sit and listen to people who have gotten into trouble with drugs, stealing, vandalism— pretty much everything. I really do regret what I did. I was just really hungry and tired of eating fruit snacks and Top Ramen.

My mom removes her reading glasses and sets them down on the table. "Grey, I really don't like the idea of you getting a job, especially when you're struggling in school."

I glance down at Luna's phone number on my hand. I

felt like a dumbass when I had to write it down. I knew Luna was wondering why I didn't just enter it into my phone. I didn't lie to her about my friends breaking it. But the incident happened a couple of weeks ago, and right now, there's no money to replace it, so I'm stuck using the house phone.

"We need the money." I tear open a fruit snack bag, tip my head back, and empty the whole pouch into my mouth. "And I found someone to tutor me. We're starting today, so I either need to borrow the car or need someone to give me a ride to the library later tonight."

"Tutoring sounds expensive. Maybe I can help you."

"I love you, Mom. I really do. But you've tried to help me with my homework before, and you always end up getting pissed off. And the person who's tutoring isn't really a tutor. She's just a …" I'm not sure what to call Luna. Up until the other day when I saw her steal from Benny's store, we barely spoke to each other, even if we have gone to the same school since kindergarten. We're definitely not close, but at the same time, I feel like she might understand my situation. "She's just a friend, not an actual hired tutor."

"Oh, okay." She relaxes a bit. "That was really nice of her."

"Yeah, it is." I'm not surprised Luna agreed to help me, even with what happened our sophomore year. She's just that way—really nice and sweet, something I'm not used to.

Stuffing the rest of the fruit snacks into my pocket, I wander back to my room to put my books on my bed. Then I pull out the envelope Beckett gave me. I'm still unsure what I'm going to do with the money inside— whether I'm going to spend it or not. I want back what I gave up for it, but my family needs the help. And once I spend it, what I gave to Beck will be gone forever.

I hide the envelope under my mattress where my mom won't find it then leave my room. I yell bye to my mom then head out the front door before she can say anything to me. She's been so stressed out over the last few months, and I hate that she now has to worry over her son's life falling apart.

I'm trying to get my shit together—get my grades up, get a job, and start paying for my own stuff. If I wasn't such a spoiled brat to begin with, the change might not have been so hard. But up until my father got sick, and even a little bit after, I was a cocky asshole who always got his way and who did things—really bad things—that they got away with, even though they shouldn't. I'm trying not to be that person anymore, because I get it now—what it feels like to have the whole world against you sometimes. And what it feels like to be truly ashamed of the person you are.

"You're a good son, Grey," were my dad's final words

to me. He looked up at me from his bed, pale and thin, just bones and skin, as he clasped my hand. "I'm so proud of the man you've become."

He was so wrong. I wasn't a good person. I was someone who stood around and watched people get bullied and who did it himself sometimes. I did awful things. And I let my dad die, thinking I was the opposite. I didn't even have the balls to tell him the truth.

I take a deep breath as I wind around the corner of the block to the main street that runs through town. I wipe my eyes before I pick up my pace for the entrance door, noting the time on the town clock and realizing I'm early.

I slam to a stop when I spot Luna walking up the sidewalk in my direction with an older woman and man at her side. Either they're her parents or her grandparents. I can't tell because they look older, at least sixty or so.

Luna looks different than she does at school, more tense and depressed. She isn't wearing the shorts and tank top she had on earlier, the ones that show off her long, lean legs and smooth skin. I remember the first day she came to school dressed differently. It was toward the beginning of junior year, and everyone was talking about it. Some people were making fun of how she got the clothes.

"She must have robbed a store or something," I

remember Piper saying. "Seriously, there's no way she can go from thrift store shit to designer."

I didn't say anything, only nodded. I hardly ever said much, which didn't make me any better than the rest of them.

Not everyone was rude about it, though. I remember a couple of my friends talking about her "hot ass." She does have a hot ass, and those legs of hers go on for miles. But the outfit she has on now covers all of that up.

"I still can't believe what you've done," the woman seethes at her as she jerks open the door to the building I'm supposed to go into. "You know better than to have those kinds of things. After everything I've taught you, you should know better. You shouldn't want that kind of stuff."

Luna enters the building, biting her nails, and the woman and man go inside with her.

I briefly contemplate the idea of ditching the therapy session and just going home. The last thing I want is for people at school to find out what I did or why I did it. I don't think Luna is the kind of person to tell anyone, though, so I crack my knuckles, square my shoulders, and pull the door open.

The woman is still chewing out Luna as I enter. Thankfully, no one else has arrived, because she's making a scene, and Luna looks horrified enough without an audience.

"It's ridiculous that we're even here," she snaps, standing on her tiptoes to get in Luna's face.

The man remains close to Luna, backing her into a corner, as if they're trying to make "intimidate Luna" a team effort.

"I can't believe my daughter has to come to a place like this, but you need to learn your lesson because my punishments clearly aren't working. Hopefully, this place will give you some insight to how you're going to end up if you keep heading in this direction. You know what kinds of people come to these meeting, Luna? Drug addicts, thieves, whores. They're just like your aunt Ashlynn. Is that how you want to end up, Luna? Do you want to be whore? Because those clothes and makeup I found make you look like one."

Whoa. This woman is intense.

I contemplate backing out of the room and waiting outside or maybe even stepping in and stopping them, but the man glances in my direction and gives me a judgmental look that pisses me off. I carry his gaze, daring him to say something to me. He glares back before looking away.

Yeah, douchebag, look away.

The woman—Luna's mom—fiddles with Luna's hair and tugs on the bottom of her sweatshirt that already reaches her knees. Then she does the same to her own hair and button down shirt.

"You have exactly ten minutes to get home after the meeting ends. If you're late, you'll get punished, do you understand?"

"Yes," Luna mutters with her eyes fixed on the carpet.

"I'd pick you up myself, but your father and I have a church meeting," she continues. "Your phone better show you at home at five ten."

"I said I understand." Luna squeezes her eyes shut.

"This is your own fault," the man, who I assume is her dad, says in an icy tone. "You did this to yourself by making the wrong choices that have embarrassed this family. Think about that while you're here. You've been such a terrible person. If you keep going down this road, do you know where that's going to get you in life? Nowhere, that's where. Losers stay losers, Luna, so stop being one."

With that, the two of them turn to leave. As they pass me, the man gives me another nasty look, and the woman's eyes narrow on me.

"See? That's the kind of people who belong here," she whispers loudly enough for me to hear. "He looks like a troublemaker."

"I think that's Gary Sawyer's son," the man replies as he shoves open the door. "So that's no surprise."

Hearing him talk about my dad that way makes me want to beat his ass. My dad was a good person, who yeah, let me get away with more shit than he should've, but he never yelled at me and tried to intimidate me by telling me I'm a bad person.

Getting into a fight with an old dude is the last thing I should be doing, though, so I curl my hands into fists and focus on breathing until the two of them leave the building.

"Goddammit," Luna curses as she yanks off the sweatshirt and tosses it on the floor. "Why do they have to be my parents? Why? Why? Why?" She stomps on the shirt several times before she notices me. Then her cheeks turn red. "What are you doing here?" She crinkles her nose as if the idea thoroughly disgusts her.

"Probably for the same reason you're here." I point at the circle of fold up chairs in the middle of the room. "For the session."

"Oh, yeah... Right." She scoops up the sweatshirt from the floor. "How long have you been standing there?"

I pretend to be casual, even though I just witnessed her parents rip into her. "Not too long."

She assesses me as she ties the shirt around her waist. "You saw them yelling at me, didn't you?"

I offer her an apologetic shrug. "How'd you know?"

She readjusts the bottom of her tank top that was hidden under the sweatshirt. "Because I know that look on your face. You feel sorry for me. Wynter gets the same look on her face every time she sees my parents get mad at me." She pauses. "Thanks, though, for trying to lie about it to spare me the embarrassment."

"You shouldn't be embarrassed. They should."

She eyes me over warily. "Even after the temper tantrum I just threw?"

"I would've lost my shit, too." I step toward her. "I would've yelled at them, though."

"I wish I did." She frowns, unconvinced, and then forces a laugh that sounds all kinds of wrong. "I guess you just got a glimpse of what I can be like when I lose games, right?"

I don't say anything. I'm not sure what to say. She's embarrassed, but I don't want her to be. I want her to feel comfortable around me, especially since we're going to be spending time together while she tutors me.

She stares at the floor. "I'm sorry you had to see that. My parents are just really intense, especially when I mess up."

"I get it," I say, though I don't. Yeah, my mom and dad have gotten pissed off at me when I have gotten into trouble, but they usually just ground me.

"Do you?" she mumbles, staring off into empty space. "Because I don't."

"Everyone's parents get pissed at them sometimes," I tell her in an attempt to make her feel better.

"But does everyone's parents haul them to a group therapy session because they found makeup and nail polish and worry they're going to turn into a prostitute?" she challenges then shakes her head. "I'm so sorry. I shouldn't be talking to you about this. You don't need to hear about my problems."

"You're fine. You can say whatever you want. I swear I won't tell anyone." I mean it, too. I owe her for what I did to her in tenth grade, and now might be my chance to make up for how horribly I treated her.

Apparently, she doesn't believe I'm being that genuine, because uncomfortable silence stretches between us.

"They really brought you here because they think you're a prostitute?" I ask, breaking the silence.

"They think makeup leads to prostitution. And nail polish. And stupid, lacy, black panties." She rolls her eyes. "Like that's actually a thing."

Black, lacy panties? Is that what she has on under there? My gaze deliberately sweeps over her long legs hidden by those loose jeans, her narrow waist, her chest, her lips …

I tear myself from my lustful thoughts as she peers up at me through her eyelashes, looking as innocent as can be.

Okay, how the hell can her parents think she's going to turn into a prostitute? She's, like, the sweetest girl ever.

"You thought I was here because I shoplifted, didn't you?" she asks, fiddling with the hem of her shirt.

"No," I lie. That's exactly what I thought.

She continues to nervously wring the bottom of her shirt, pulling it high enough that I catch a glimpse of the bottom of her flat stomach. "It should be." She swiftly shakes her head. "I'm sorry I'm dumping all this crap on you. I think I'm just stressed out or something. We don't know each other. You don't need to hear about my problems."

"But you do know me." I offer her a lopsided smile that seems to fluster her. "We've been in the same school together for practically forever."

"Yeah, but up until the thing at … Benny's"—she winces—"We've only said, like, maybe ten words to each other, ever since … well, you know."

"So what if we didn't used to talk? We're talking now. You can talk to me about whatever you want. Isn't that why we're at this place? To talk about our problems?" God, I sound like an idiot.

She must think so too because she just stares at me for a heartbeat or two, looking really suspicious. Then she sits down in one of the chairs and pulls out her phone from the pocket of her sweatshirt.

Okay, I guess that's the end of our conversation then.

I watch her mess around with her phone for a bit. Her head is down; her long, brown hair concealing her face; and her shoulders are hunched over. While she's usually a little bit quiet, she isn't this openly offish.

When I finally sit down beside her, she doesn't glance up at me, but I feel her tense as my shoulder brushes hers.

"Everything okay?" I ask, trying to get her to look up at me.

"Yep." She clears her throat as she scoots over an inch.

It throws me off a little. Usually, girls move closer to me, not away. I guess I deserve it from her.

Her eyes remain on her phone, her fingers scrolling through texts messages. I try not to read what's on the screen, but it's hard not to glance down every once in a while.

Ari: So, if you bring your phone to school tomorrow and give it to me for a couple of hours, I can swap out phones. U can have a backup to take with you and one to leave wherever. That way, your parents can still get ahold of u whenever, but they won't know where u r. Or they'll think you're at wherever your phone is, anyway.

Jesus, her parents are way beyond intense. It makes me feel even shittier for the stuff my friends put her through. Not only did she have to suffer through them teasing her, but she had to go home and deal with her parents.

She types a response.

Luna: Thank you! You're the best. And I don't want to be all needy or anything, but what about the other thing?

Ari: I'm still working on it. Tracking a number is a bit more complicated then messing around with an app.

Tracking a phone number? What the hell?

Luna: Awesome! Again, you're the bestest of bestest. And the smartest and the funniest and the most clever,

Ari: Aw, you're making me blush, Lu.

She smiles at that then taps open another message,

Wynter: A new band I found that I think you'll love. It's not mix music or anything, but it's got a good beat to it. Cheer up, girly. We've all got your back. Always and forever.

I feel the slightest bit jealous of Luna and her friends and how much they seem to care about each other. Mine give me nothing but shit for getting put on academic probation. I can't even imagine telling them about my other problems.

Although, the whole tracking numbers and messing up app thing is a little weird.

Is that a normal thing for friends to do?

Luna clicks on an audio file titled "There's No 'I' In Team" by Taking Back Sunday, and a song blasts through the speaker of her phone. She casts a glance around the empty room then at me.

"Is it cool if I listen to this?" she tasks.

"You're fine. In fact, turn it up."

"Yeah?"

"Yeah. I like music."

She considers this like it's something questionable, which makes me wonder what she thinks of me.

"All right." She relaxes as she cranks up the music and sings along.

Apparently, she already knows the song. I lean back in the chair, stretching out my legs, and tap my fingers to the beat. She smiles at me when she notices my fingers drumming against my knees, and I return her smile. It's probably the most content I've felt in weeks, and part of me wishes the song would keep playing forever so the moment would never have to end.

Like everything else, it does, and the room eventually grows quiet again.

"Does Wynter always send you songs to cheer you up?" I ask.

"How'd you know this was from Wynter?" she questions suspiciously, setting her phone down on her lap. "Did you read my messages?"

"Um..." Crap. I could lie, but I can't even come up with a good one right now. So, not seeing any other choice, I tell the truth, which might be a first for me in quite a while. "I didn't mean to read them. They were just kind of there, you know. And I'm kind of fascinated by you and your friends."

Her brow cocks. "You mean my *intimidating* friends?"

I seriously can't tell if she's teasing me or not.

"I've decided they're just intimidating to outsiders," I tell her. "They seem like good friends."

"They are," she assures me. "They've always been there for me."

"It's good you have them. I'm kind of jealous."

"Of *me*?" Again, she gets that questioning look in her eyes.

I nod and twist in the chair, facing her. "I just think it'd be nice to have friends I can tell anything to without worrying they'll make fun of me."

"I don't tell my friends everything," she admits. "Not because I think they'd make fun of me or anything—I know they'd never do that. There's just some things I'm embarrassed of … like the thing you saw me do the other day." She stares at me like she's trying to unraveling a mystery. "You know, the thing you know about me that no one else does."

"You shouldn't be embarrassed about that. I really do understand." More than I want to tell you.

"Why I stole … It's not as simple as you think." Her head angles to the side as a contemplative look crosses her face. "Can I …? Do you care if I …?" She looks away from me. "Never mind."

"No, go ahead. Say what you're going to say. The guy who runs this thing is going to be here soon, anyway, and he's going to ask everyone a shitload of questions."

She crinkles her freckled nose for the second time in

fifteen minutes and I decide it might be the most adorable thing I've ever seen. "Really?"

I nod. "But you don't have to answer them if you don't want to."

"I wish I didn't have to talk at all," she grimaces.

"I think a lot of people here are the same way. It's hard talking about your problems, isn't it?"

She eyes me over closely. "How long have you been coming to these meetings?" she asks.

"A few weeks." Should I say anything about why I'm here? You know what? Screw it. She's going to find out sooner or later. "I was caught stealing from Mountain Ridge Grocery, and the owner, Larry, said he wouldn't press charges just as long as I came to a month's worth of meetings."

"You were caught stealing?" she questions, like she's not quite sure she believes me.

"Yeah... It was really stupid. I don't know why I thought I could get away with it. My shirt looked so bulky."

"What'd you take?" she asks curiously

I pick at a tiny hole in the knee of my jeans. "Soda, chips, and a steak."

She seems unfazed by my confession, which makes me wonder just how many times she has stolen.

"Was it the first time you ever stole?"

I nod. "What about you? Was that day at Benny's your first time?"

She shakes her head with her lips fused.

"I'm sure you have a good reason for doing it, though," I add.

"Did I?" she mutters, opening and flexing her fingers as she stares down at the scars on her hands.

I open my mouth to apologize for even bringing this up, but I can't figure out the right words or if there are any right words. A simple sorry doesn't feel right, not after all the stuff we did to her, the things we said. Logan even spread a rumor that her body was covered with the same scars she has on her hands. He never explained how he could possibly know that, but no one cared. They only believed it.

"What happened?" I ask, grazing my fingers along her palm.

She stretches out her fingers. "Our house caught on fire when I was four, and I was stuck in my room for a while. I got the scars when I was crawling across the floor, trying to get out. There are a couple on my knees, too, but they're really hard to see."

My throat suddenly feels thick as her words remind me of a memory I refuse to think of, but is now pressing against the surface of my mind. "Wow, that had to be scary."

She gives a half-shrug. "I can't really remember what

happened. Sometimes, when I'm asleep, I dream I'm crawling across the floor in the middle of flames, and then someone scoops me up, but that's about all I can remember."

I reach out and trace my fingers along the scars again. "Did it hurt? I mean, when your hands were burned?"

"Yeah, it did. That part, I do remember."

I stroke her palm again, wondering how long she'll let me touch her before she pulls away. Hopefully, she'll let me for a while, because I find the movement comforting, like we're connecting somehow. Or maybe it's because I'm having an actual, real conversation.

"How'd the fire start?" I ask quietly.

She shrugs. "From what my parents say, someone started a fire in the fireplace that spread throughout the house."

My chest feels extremely tight. "So it was started intentionally?"

"That's the story. The police never did find out who did it."

"You say that like you don't buy the whole story."

She wavers her head from side to side while chewing on her bottom lip. "Sometimes, I don't... Maybe because when I dream about what happened, I can remember being carried out of the house. The thing is, my parents say a fireman rescued me, but I swear it feels like I knew the person ... I felt so safe in their arms ..." She shakes her head. "But, anyway, I'm probably remembering things wrong since I was so little."

I trace the tip of my finger down one of the longer, angular scars, trying to focus on the conversations, but images of flames stream through my mind. "Have you ever told your parents about the dreams?"

She nods. "They're the ones who told me I'm probably remembering wrong. They said there was no way I could remember something that happened when I was four years old and that I should just be glad the fireman got me out of the house. They do that a lot—try to tell me how to think."

"I'm not surprised," I say. "Have they always been that way? So … intense?"

"Pretty much." She rotates in her seat so we're both facing inward and our knees are only inches apart. "One of my first memories is of them collecting all my toys, bagging them up, and throwing them in the trash. Then I got this big lecture on how I was too old to play with toys, and it was time to grow up and start learning to behave properly. I was five when she did that."

"You were *five*? That's fucking crazy. My younger sister's eleven, and she still has a toy box and everything."

"That's just one of the many stories when I felt like I had to grow up too fast." Her expression unexpectedly fills with worry. "I don't even know why I'm telling you all of this. I don't usually talk about this with anyone except my friends, and that's only because they've seen my parents do"—she flicks her wrist, motioning behind us where her parents reamed into her moments ago —"what you saw them do."

"I told you that you could talk to me. And I like listening to you talk." I like having an actual conversation that carries depth.

"Really? Why? My stories are so ..."

"Real? Honest?"

"I was going to go with messed up."

"Still, they're real. I haven't had a real conversation in a long time." *Since my father died.* "Whenever I'm with my friends, they always want to talk about sports or who they screwed around with at last weekend's party. And Piper ... All she wants to talk about is the dance and what party we're going to hit up." I stop myself as Luna's demeanor shifts. "Are you okay?"

"Yeah, I'm fine." She tries to shrug it off, but I can tell that she's lying and that something is bothering her. My bet is Piper did something to Luna. I wouldn't be surprised since I've seen Piper do a lot of messed up shit to people over the last year while I was dating her, and I just stood by and watched.

"So, you have a little sister, huh?" she asks. "That's got to be nice, not being the only child."

"It's nice sometimes, but she can be a pain in the ass when she doesn't get her way." Although, she has been quieter lately, which is why I've been trying to spend more time with her.

"Still, it's better than being the only child and being the sole focus for your parents." Her phone hums from her lap, but she doesn't pick it up.

"I've never looked at it that way, but I get what you're saying," I reply. "There's been a ton of times I've gotten away with stuff because Mia had my parents distracted with something she did."

"Do you guys do a lot of stuff together?"

"We didn't used to, but ever since … my father died, I feel like I need to spend more time with her."

"That has to be hard, losing your dad."

"It was—is hard." I pretend to have an itch on the corner of my eye to cover up the tears trying to escape. "He was really involved in my life. He's actually the reason I'm so into sports. When I was about four, he started taking me to soccer games, baseball games, football—pretty much every single sport you can think of. When I started playing sports myself, he never missed any of my games, and he was the same way with Mia. She was really into dance for a while, and he always went to her recitals."

"He sounds like a good dad."

"He was the best... He had a hard time when he got sick, because he couldn't do as much stuff with Mia and me anymore. I think he did more stuff than the doctor's thought he should."

"What was he sick with?" she asks then hurriedly adds, "Never mind. You don't need to tell me if you don't feel like talking about it."

"No, it's okay. He died of cancer." I remember the day my mom and dad sat Mia and me down to tell us. It becomes harder to fight back the tears. "It was crazy. It was like, one minute, he was perfectly healthy, and the next, he was telling us that he was sick. He didn't look sick at first, but then he started chemo, and he got weaker and frailer until he didn't even look like my dad anymore …" I trail off as my hands start to shake.

"Grey, I'm so sorry." She places a hand over mine, steadying it. "We don't have to talk about this if you don't want to."

"No, I want to," I tell her, surprised by how much I really do. "I haven't actually talked to anyone about it. Even with my mom, I don't feel comfortable because I'm afraid she's going to cry, and Mia is the same way. Every time I bring him up, she gets upset. And my friends … None of them are good listeners like you are, and they make me feel bad whenever I bring it up because they think I'm being too depressing."

"Well, I'm here if you ever want to talk."

I open my mouth to tell her that I'd really like to talk more, but the door swings open, and five people wander in, putting an end to probably the most honest conversation I've ever had.

It grows quiet between us after that and Luna returns to texting on her phone. Feeling a little unsettled about how truthful I was to her, I get up to go grab a snack from the snacks table. The selection is quite lovely, let me tell you. Some burnt chocolate chip cookies, gooey, undercooked browns, and some punch that has lumps it in. I decide to go with a pink frosting cupcake because it's literally the most delicious looking thing there. It's also the last one.

Once I collect it, I head back to my chair, sitting down right as the guy in charge walks in.

"All right everyone," he announces, let's get started.

There's a few groans, but Luna remains quiet. So do I, focusing on eating the cupcake.

I manage to wolf it down in six bites then get up to toss the wrapper in the trash. Right before I do, I notice a piece of paper stuck in the bottom of it.

Weird.

I pull it out and open it, figuring it's like a fortune or something. If it is, though, it's the most ominous one ever.

I know what you did three summers ago.

And just like that my chest feels tight again, like it did when Luna was talking about the fire.

No, there's no way. This has to be a weird freakin'

coincidence. Because no one knows about what I did. Well, my friends do, but it's not like they'd bring it up since we vowed to never talk about it again. Plus, why would they go through all the trouble of baking a cupcake to put the note at the bottom of it, then putting here at this place, and then hoping I get up to eat it?

No, this has to be a freakish coincidence. It has to be.

Still, I pocket the note and take my seat again.

Luna glances at me and frowns. "Is everything okay?"

I put on my best fake smile, something I'm good at. "Yeah, of course. I'm always okay," I lie, another thing I'm good at.

I'm also good at covering up secrets, something three summers ago proves. Or well, I thought I was. But if this note has any truth to it...

I'm so screwed.

LUNA

When I was fourteen, I stole a jacket when my mom was taking me school clothes shopping. It wasn't even a jacket I liked. It was too big and bulky and a horrible shade of puke green.

Right before I jacked it, I was following my mom around the store, watching her put clothes in the cart that I was supposed to wear while listening to her ridicule every person around us.

"Oh, look at that girl, Luna." She pointed at a girl around my age who was wearing a tight black dress, matching boots, and had a stud through her nose. "Imagine how she'll end up in a few years. Probably on the corner of a street." She didn't even say it quietly, and the girl gave us a nasty look.

I was beyond mortified and wanted to say something,

but I kept my mouth shut, knowing she'd punish me if I smarted off. But I felt something silently snap inside me, break, and I stole for the very first time in my life. For the briefest second, I felt in control, like I was somehow yelling fuck you to my mom without actually saying the words aloud.

After I made it out of the store with the jacket, I gave it to a homeless woman standing near the store, like somehow that made me a better person. It didn't.

I've known what kind of person I am ever since I was seven years old, and my parents tried to explain to me how I was supposed to act, what I was supposed to wear, and who I was supposed to be. I remember thinking it didn't sound like someone I wanted to be, which had to make me a bad person.

I spend most of the session listening to the rest of the group talk about their problems while silently drowning in my own. I desperately want to steal something. My hands twitch to snatch something up and hide it in my pocket. I long for control, long to breathe for two goddamn seconds. But I can't go anywhere.

Or can I?

I glance at the exit door several times, debating whether to get up and make a quick trip to the store. I could be in and out in five minutes. What if my parents found out I left, though? All it would take is for one of their church friends to spot me, and word would get back to them.

What do I do?

What kind of person am I to be sitting here, contemplating this?

I'm so messed up.

My head is crammed with thoughts that are in no way related to the session, and I can barely think straight. Maybe I would've ran out too if I didn't receive a text.

Unknown: Look at you, finally paying for all of your punishments.

Awesome. Douchebag unknown caller is back.

I haven't heard from them since earlier today in the bathroom when they may have speculated that they told my parents about my hiding spot beneath the floorboards. The thing is only my friends know about that spot—although, they think I purchased everything I hide in there—and I know none of them out my secret, so either the texter wasn't really implying that they told my parents or... Well, somehow someone found out about my hiding spot. But that leaves the big old question: how? Ari had suggested that maybe someone hacked my phone, but then that leaves the question: Why? Yeah, I'm chock full of questions today. And restlessness. And confusion.

I want to send a text back to the person, but Howard,

the guy in charge, asks me, "Luna... That's your name, right?"

Great. I hate being put on the spot.

I nod. "Yeah."

"That's a cool name," he tells me. "Way better than plain old Howard."

I force a smile, noting how Grey covers up his mouth, I think to stifle a laugh. "Yeah, it's pretty cool."

He smiles. "Well, Luna with the cool name, would you like to tell everyone why you're here."

I glance around at everyone staring at me. "Do I have to?"

"No. Not today. But eventually, to pass the class, you will have to open up." He keeps on smiling. "But no pressure."

Right, Howard with the uncool name, there's no pressure at all.

But thankfully, he moves on, to Grey of all people, asking him to share his feelings about what he did. Grey does too and he makes it look easy, telling the truth. But Grey isn't a liar like me.

"I felt bad about what I did," Grey tells everyone. "No matter why I stole the stuff, it wasn't fair to just take it from someone else, you know? But it felt like this other person took over and let me justify putting that stuff in my pocket. But I don't think that makes me a bad person." He cast a sidelong glance at me.

It feels like he's trying to send me a message, like he gets me. I wish he did. Maybe then I could finally open up to someone and release the pressure building in my chest instead of having to steal in order to do so. He doesn't understand me, though, even if he thinks he does.

Grey has stolen a total of one time, and I'm guessing it was just a rebellious act to get a rush. He doesn't understand what it's like to go to the store with the sole purpose of stealing, what it's like to feel like you have to do it; otherwise, your entire world will spin out of control. He isn't sitting here, contemplating running out the door just so he can put something in his pocket to get some messed up form of temporary peace. And the only reason he doesn't is because he might have someone potentially blackmailing him?

Reality bitch smacks me across the face. Wait, is that what's going on with this?

My fingers itch to look at the message again, but someone is talking and looking at Grey who's sitting beside me and I know it'd be totally obvious if I looked at my phone right now.

"I totally get what you're saying," a woman in her mid-twenties with short, black hair says. "It's like when I used to get high. I'd always justify what I was doing, but after I crashed, I always felt so fucking bad about what I did. I don't think what I did made me a bad person; I just made bad fucking choices. I wish my sister could see how hard

I'm trying and forgive me. I know I did a lot of terrible shit to her, but I've been trying to get my shit together, you know?"

"Give her some time," Howard says. "I know it's hard, but like with how you're still healing over your addiction, your sister needs time to heal, too."

The woman nods, anxiously thrumming her fingers on her knees. "I hope so. I really do ... I miss her."

I think about my own parents at home and wonder if they'll ever forgive me for the stuff they discovered about me today. I doubt it. They were already upset from finding the stuff. And when they asked me how I got the money to pay for everything, I couldn't come up with an answer, and they somehow put two and two together.

"You stole it, didn't you?" my mom asked, but it wasn't a question. Somehow, she just knew her daughter was a thief. "I should've seen this coming."

"This is partly your fault." My dad put some of the blame on my mom, which surprised me. Usually, they blamed me for everything. "Clearly, you haven't been controlling her enough."

"I've been trying"—she slammed her fist against the table—"but she's uncontrollable. She doesn't do what she's told. I don't think I can help her anymore."

Shock ricocheted through me. Never in my life had I seen her so ... out of control.

"Well, she definitely doesn't get that from my side of

the family," he said, shoving his chair back from the table to stand up. "Find a way to fix her."

I expected her to make me burn all the stuff she found, but I should've known it wouldn't be that easy.

Going to the sessions for a week is only the start. I'm also not allowed out of the house except to go to school, to the sessions, and to the library for an hour a day. The last part was only a stipulation because I told my mom I had a school project to work on that required after school time with a group and that we're supposed to meet up at the library. Part of me lied just so I could get a break from the house, but I also didn't want to back out of tutoring Grey when I promised him I would.

But that's not my biggest problem. I'm basically on my parents' version of house arrest, which means I'll be around them more, which means I'm going to want to steal more but won't have a chance to. Not that I can if whoever is texting me is watching me.

Crap. What am I going to do? How am I going to deal with this?

"Luna, the session is over."

I blink out of my trance. To my surprise, almost everyone has cleared out of the room.

Holy crap, talking about zoning off.

Grey is standing in front of me with concern in his eyes. "You kind of zoned out. Are you okay?"

I glance at the time and realize I have five minutes to get home. The only way I'll make it is if I run.

"Shit, I'm going to be late." I spring from the chair.

Grey has zero time to move out of my way, and my chest collides with his as my forehead knocks into his chin.

"Shit," he curses as he trips back, clutching his chin.

I slap my hand over my mouth. "Oh, my God, I'm so sorry."

"It's fine." His face is contorted in pain as he rubs his chin.

I glance from the door to him. Crap, crap, crap, I'm gonna be late if I don't haul ass home now. "Are you sure?"

"Yeah, I'm positive." He lowers his hand, and his lips tug into a joking smile. "You have a really hard head, though."

I let out an edgy laugh, my gaze darting to the door again. "I know I'm going to sound like a jerk, but I have to get home, like, right now or my mom's going to freak out."

"You don't sound like a jerk, and I swear I'm okay." He waves at me to go.

I shoot him a grateful look then rush for the door. "Sorry I bumped you in the head," I call out.

He strides with me, flattening his palm against the

door to open it for me. "Are you still going to be able to make it to the library tonight? It's okay if you can't."

I shake my head as I speed walk toward the corner of the street. "No, I can make it. I told my parents I have a group project I have to work on." I pause at the end of the sidewalk, deciding which route is the quickest. "Which way's faster?" I mutter, dragging my fingers through my hair.

"Where do you live?" Grey appears by my side. I tell him my address, and he ponders something for a second before he veers to the right. "Come on. I know a shortcut."

I run after him, my sneakers thudding against the concrete. "One that will get me home in three minutes?"

"That all depends."

"On what?"

He shoots me a challenging grin. "On how fast you run."

He takes off, and I race after him. People walking through the neighborhood openly gawk at us as we sprint past them, laughing. When the sidewalk reaches a dead end, Grey doesn't slow down, running straight for a six-foot, wooden fence that separates the neighborhood from a small tree area. He stops when he reaches the fence and crouches down with his hands linked.

"Hop on, and I'll boost you up," he says, barely out of breath.

I trip to a stop, gasping for air. *I really need to start exercising more.*

"Are you sure? I don't want to hurt you."

He gives me an are-you-kidding-me look. "I think I can handle it."

I prop my foot into his hands and grasp the top of the fence. He grunts as he stands up and hoists me up. I get my balance then jump down onto the other side, landing in the dirt on my hands and knees. Then I trip to my feet and stumble for the trees.

I hear a soft thump behind me as I barrel into the trees. I glance over my shoulder and see Grey jogging after me.

"What? Did you think I was just going to let you wander into the forest by yourself when it's almost sundown?" he teases as he gets ahead of me and runs backward down a dirt path that cuts straight through the trees. "What kind of a guy do you think I am?"

"I have no idea." I might have thought I had an idea, but I'm not so sure anymore.

Honestly, I'm not sure about anything, something I realize as I receive a text from unknown again. I don't slow down as I read the message.

Unknown: Tick, tock. Tick, tock. Who's about to get into trouble?

Grr... This person is getting on my nerves.

"Is everything okay?" Grey asks, studying my expression closely.

"Um... yeah," I lie as I pocket my phone, my heart racing in my chest. Who is this person and why are they trying to torment me? "How do you know about this shortcut?"

"I take it home sometimes," he answers, glancing at the path ahead.

"I thought you drove your truck to school?" I ask, but instantly realize my mistake.

He glances out of the corner of his eye at me. "How do you know I drive a truck?"

I give him what I hope is an indifferent shrug. "Doesn't everyone in this town know what everyone drives?"

"Yeah, I guess." His head tilts back as he gazes up at the pale pink sky. "I don't have my truck anymore." Pain is in his eyes. "I sold it when my dad died. It was hard, because he was the one who gave me the truck."

"I'm so sorry. That had to be hard."

"It was, but we needed the money." His gaze fastens on mine. "No one's noticed I don't have my truck anymore, not even my friends."

"Not even Logan?" I ask breathlessly as I swat branches out of my way.

He shakes his head. "Logan's a self-centered dick. The

only way he'd notice is if he suddenly needed a ride somewhere."

"What about Piper?"

A hollow laugh leaves his lips. "Yeah, Piper and Logan are kind of the same way. It's okay, though. I'd rather them not notice. Then I don't have to tell them why I had to sell it."

"I get what you're saying," I pant out, wiping the sweat from my brow. "I don't talk to my friends about everything. I love them to death, but sometimes, I worry about stuff."

He hops over a log blocking the path. "Worry about what exactly?"

"That they won't love some of the things that I do … won't understand why I do the things I do." I dodge around a pothole in the path then turn to my side right as a revelation smacks me across the face.

Crappity crap. Grey is going to see the home I live in and know I'm not stealing because my family lives in poverty.

I search for an excuse that will get him to turn around and go home before we make it to my house. Before I can think of a good lie, though, the trees thin and my two-story home with a lavish front yard and three car garage comes into view.

Silence sets in as he takes in where we're at. "You live here?" he questions.

"Um... Yeah." I feel like the biggest fake ever.

Silence settles between us. An awkward kind that makes me squirm. I dare a glance in his direction then cringe at the disgust in his eyes, the same disgust he had the day he turned me down for the dance.

"Thanks for telling me about the shortcut." I pick up the pace, even though my legs are furious with me.

He doesn't come after me, which is good since I'm pretty sure I won't be able to look him in the eye ever again.

I make it home with seconds to spare, getting the door shut right before my mom calls.

I know I should feel grateful that I made it home in time and avoided further punishments, but all I feel is trapped and in desperate need to get control again. I can't breathe. I swear the walls are about to close in and crush me to death.

And that feeling only grows as I get another text.

Unknown: Made it home just in time. I'd say be relieved, but we both know you have a ton of secrets just waiting to get out.

Me: Who is this?

Unknown: For now, I'm going to keep that to myself. Just know that I know all about you, Luna, including who really started that fire.

Confusion webs through my veins.

Me: Who?

Unknown: You don't know the answer already?

Me: No. Tell me who.

Unknown: Nah. I think I'm going to sit on this one for a while. Talk to you soon.

Me: Tell me who it is!

But they don't answer.

Gritting my teeth, I text Ari.

Me: You haven't by chance found out who it is yet, have you?

Ari: I'm still looking into it. Whoever it is, knows what they're doing because they've got a ton of security on their phone.

I blow out a frustrated exhale. Why would someone just randomly do this to me? Did I do something to piss someone off?

I'm not sure, but I'm going to find out no matter what it takes. Not just because I refuse to be blackmailed, but because I want to know who started that fire.

GREY

LUNA DOESN'T SHOW up at the library. With how horrified she looked when she ran away from me, I'm not surprised. I could see in her eyes that she thought I was judging her, and why wouldn't she think that? It's not like I have a great track record of being a nice, nonjudgmental guy.

But I wasn't judging her. While I don't fully understand why she stole, I don't think she's a bad person. After I saw how her parents treat her, I think I understand why she thinks she's, though.

I call her when I get home, but she doesn't answer, so I end up asking my mom for help with my English paper, which turns into a disaster. She freaks out when she discovers that the assignment is about Shakespeare's work.

124

"But I haven't read anything by him."

"Me, either," I tell her, trying to make her feel better.

She scowls at me from across the kitchen table. "You're telling me you haven't been doing the reading assignments?"

"I tried, but I could barely make it through the first scene." I lower my head into my hands. "I feel like an idiot. I shouldn't have waited until my senior year to try to get my grades up."

"Honey, you're not an idiot, and I don't want you to ever say that again." She reaches across the table and tugs on my arm until I look at her. "We'll get your grades up."

I force a smile, hoping she's right, that somehow she can help me make good on the promise to be a better person. Getting my grades up is part of accomplishing that.

I wish I hadn't screwed around so much for the last few years. Then maybe reading Shakespeare wouldn't be like trying to understand Latin.

"What happened with the girl who was supposed to tutor you?" Mom asks as she reads over the assignment sheet again.

"She had something come up and couldn't make it," I lie as my stomach grumbles.

My mom glances at me then at the clock. "Wow, I didn't even realize it was that late. I should make dinner." She pushes back from the table, wanders over to the cupboard, and takes out three cans of Ravioli. "Why don't you call her and see if maybe she can meet you another day?"

My hunger pains increase at the sight of the cans. "That might work." But I'm not sure Luna would be too happy to help me after what happened unless I somehow convince her that I'm not the douchebag I used to be.

"Mom, can I ask you a question?"

"Of course, honey," she says as she presses the can opener into the top of the can.

I pick at the cracks in the table. "Say there was this person who was an asshole to someone for a really long time. Then one day something happened, and he decided he needed to change, but the girl he wanted to be friends with was someone he did some messed up stuff to. How would he go about convincing this girl that he's not a jerk anymore?"

She narrows her eyes at me as she rotates the handle on the opener. "Grey Sawyer, have you been mean to girls?"

"Not lately … But, yeah, I have … in the past," I confess, ashamed.

I'm ashamed of a lot of things, like what I did those few years ago during the summer.

I'd tried to shove it out of my mind and have been doing a somewhat decent job until I read that stupid weird fortune that was at the bottom of the cupcake.

She pries the lid off the can. "I thought I raised you better than that."

"You did. I just didn't listen to all the amazing stuff you taught me." I try to dazzle her with my most charming smile.

She wags a finger at me. "Don't try to charm me, young man."

"Sorry. I'm trying to change, though … be better … be the person Dad thought I was."

She grows quiet, and when she speaks again, her voice is overflowing with emotion. "Your dad didn't *think* you were a good person. He *knew* you were."

I shake my head. "He might've thought I was, but … I've done some messed up stuff." Guilt clutches at my chest as I remember that day almost three years ago, the smoke, the flames.

She chucks the lid of the can into the trash below the sink then wipes her hands clean on a dishtowel. "Well, I guess it's time to start showing everyone the good side of you." She pulls out the trash bag from the bin and ties it up. "And you can start with taking the trash out for your mom."

I get up and take the bag from her.

As I'm heading for the back door, she says, "And, Grey, if you want to show this girl you're a nice guy, you can start by telling her you're sorry."

"You think it's that easy?"

"No, but I think it's a start."

"Okay."

I spend the rest of the evening eating dinner with Mia and my mom while trying to think of what I'm going to say to Luna tomorrow and how to apologize to her. After I eat as much as I can, scraping the plate clean, I get ready for bed then head into the office to say good night to my mom. But I stop just outside the door when I hear her talking on the phone.

"I know we're behind on the mortgage, but things have been rough lately." She pauses, and when she speaks again, her voice is wobbly like she's fighting back tears. "Fine, I understand. I'll come up with the money." She hangs up and bursts into sobs.

I give her a moment to cry before I knock on the door.

"Just a second," she says quickly. I hear her rustling around with something, and then she calls out, "Okay, you can come in."

I open the door and step in. Papers and folders are scattered all over the floor and stacked so high on the desk I can't even see the computer. She's kneeling in the center of the mess, her eyes red from crying.

"Hey, honey." She starts sorting through the papers. "Did you need something?"

"I just wanted to say good night." It's hard to see her like this—so broken down.

"Good night, sweetie." She smiles, but it looks forced.

"I start work in a few days," I remind her. "So I need to either borrow the car or get a ride there."

"Are you sure you're going to be able to handle a job?" she asks distractedly as she sifts through a small stack of papers that look like medical bills.

I lean against the doorframe. "Yes, I'm sure."

We've had this conversation at least ten times already, and I've given her the same answer. If I didn't think I could handle a job, then I wouldn't have begged Benny again today to take a risk on me. Thankfully, he took pity on me, mostly because of my father.

"Your father was a good man," he said as he struggled to turn on the computer mouse. "You know he helped me out when he was your age. It was when I first opened the store." He pounded the mouse against the counter. "Damn technology. I told Margret I didn't want an upgrade, that my system was fine, but she said it was getting too complicated without having electronic records of everything."

"Here, let me help you." I took the mouse from him, flipped it over, and turned on the power button. "It should work now," I said, handing it back to him.

He looked at the mouse dubiously then set it down on the pad and clicked it. His eyes lit up as he stared at the screen. Then he smiled at me. "Grey, you have yourself a job."

He hired me for weekends since I have school and practice on weekdays. That is, if I ever make it back on the team. Truthfully, I think I would have asked for weekdays if my college career wasn't riding on a sports scholarship.

"There it is!" my mom exclaims as she waves the paper in the air.

"What is that?" I inch into the cluttered room.

"It's the title to your father's first car." She hops over a plastic bin that's in the middle of the room and hands me the paper. "Your uncle Nate's been storing it for your dad since forever. He was going to give it to you as a graduation present, but …" She forces a lump down in her throat. "But, yeah, I thought it might be better to give it to you now."

I look down at the title. A 1966 Chevy Impala.

"We should probably just sell it," I say quietly.

"That's really up to you." When I open my mouth to protest, she adds, "Your father wanted you to have that car. If you sell it, I won't take the money. You can put it away for college. Besides, the car isn't really worth anything in the condition it's in right now."

"Does it run?"

"Kind of."

"How can something kind of run?"

"I'm not sure." She twists a strand of her hair around her finger, thinking. "How about we go and talk to Nate before school tomorrow? I can drive you there before I have to go to work, and if the car runs, you can drive it to school."

"Are you sure you'll have time to do that?"

"Of course."

"Okay. I guess that sounds good." I glance down at the title again.

My dad even signed it over to me. I don't know why, but I find myself tearing up. He must have done it when he found out he was sick.

"Honey, what's wrong?" Mom asks. "I didn't mean to upset you."

"I'm not upset." I wipe my eyes with the sleeve of my shirt as I back out of the room. "I need to get to bed." I turn to leave yet pause in the doorway. "Mom, thanks for giving me this. It … It means a lot." I leave the room before I start bawling.

When I get to my room, I take out the envelope I hid under the mattress earlier today. I thought I'd have more time to decide if I wanted to use the money, but I guess I don't.

I write my mom's name on the front of the envelope along with the message: *Someone once helped me out when I needed it, and I want to pay it forward. Hope this helps.* Then I sneak out the front door and put it in the mailbox, sealing my fate, a debt I'll now need to repay.

After I return to my room, I close the door. But only minutes later, the phone rings.

"Grey, the phone!" my mom calls out.

Wondering if it's Luna, I head out and take the phone from her. "Hello?"

"Hello, Grey." The voice on the other end sounds robotic.

"Who is this?" I ask lowly as my mom walks by me and out the kitchen.

"I'm the person who you're in debt to," they reply.

"Whatever, man." I move to hang up the phone, figuring it's a prank call.

"I know what you did three summers ago," the say. "I know about the fire you caused."

I gulp, realizing that maybe that fortune wasn't just a coincidence. "What do you want?" I hiss.

"You'll see in time," the reply. "Until then, just know that I'm watching you."

The line clicks and silence fills the air.

But I can hear my heart thudding in my chest as the memories of that day fill the air.

Flames.

Smoke.

A house wilting into ash.

But nothing compares to the sounds of the screams that filled the air.

Screams that I caused.

Dear Reader!

Thanks for reading Spies, Lies, And Cupcakes (Rebels & Misfits Detectives, #1). Hope you enjoyed the story. Please note there will also stories available that follow the lives of Luna's friends, along with more stories about Luna and Grey.

Thanks for reading!
Jessica Sorensen

ABOUT THE AUTHOR

Jessica Sorensen is a *New York Times* and *USA Today* best-selling author who lives in the snowy mountains of Wyoming. When she's not writing, she spends her time reading and hanging out with her family.

Rebels & Misfits Detectives:

Spies, Lies, & Cupcakes

Untitled (coming soon)

Signed with a Kiss Series (Honeyton Alexis):

Accepting the Deal

The Start of a Mysterious Mystery

A Truthful Kiss

Untitled (coming soon)

The Heartbreaker Society Curse:

The Heartbreaker Society Curse

The Curse of the Unordinary

Untitled (coming soon)

Enchanted Chaos Series:

Enchanted Chaos

Shimmering Chaos

Iridescent Chaos

Untitled (coming soon)

The Breathing Undead Series:

Breathing Undead Lies

Untiled (coming soon)

My Cursed Superhero Life:

Cursed

Untitled (coming soon)

Capturing Magic:

Chasing Wishes

Chasing Magic

Chasing Promises

Untitled (coming soon)

Chasing the Harlyton Sisters Series:

Chasing Hadley

Falling for Hadley

Holding onto Hadley

Untitled (coming soon)

Tangled Realms:

Forever Violet

Untitled (coming soon)

Curse of the Vampire Queen:

Tempting Raven

Enchanting Raven

Alluring Raven

Untitled (coming soon)

<u>Unraveling You Series:</u>

Unraveling You

Raveling You

Awakening You

Inspiring You

Every Single Breath

Untitled (coming soon)

<u>Unexpected Series:</u>

The Unexpected Complications of Revenge

Untitled (coming soon)

<u>Shadow Cove Series:</u>

What Lies in the Darkness

What Lies in the Dark

Untitled (coming soon)

<u>Mystic Willow Bay Series:</u>

The Secret Life of a Witch

Broken Magic

Stolen Kisses

One Wild, Crazy, Zombie Night

Magical Whispers & the Undead

Untitled (coming soon)

<u>Standalones:</u>

The Illusion of Annabella

<u>Broken City Series:</u>

Nameless

Forsaken

Oblivion

Forbidden (coming soon)

<u>Guardian Academy Series:</u>

Entranced

Entangled

Enchanted

Entice

The Forest of Shadow and Bones

Untitled (coming soon)

<u>Sunnyvale Series:</u>

The Year I Became Isabella Anders

The Year of Falling in Love

The Year of Second Chances

Untitled (coming soon)

The Coincidence Series:

The Coincidence of Callie and Kayden

The Redemption of Callie and Kayden

The Destiny of Violet and Luke

The Probability of Violet and Luke

The Certainty of Violet and Luke

The Resolution of Callie and Kayden

Seth & Greyson

The Evermore of Callie & Kayden

Untitled (coming soon)

The Secret Series:

The Prelude of Ella and Micha

The Secret of Ella and Micha

The Forever of Ella and Micha

The Temptation of Lila and Ethan

The Ever After of Ella and Micha

Lila and Ethan: Forever and Always

Untitled (coming soon)

Ella and Micha: Infinitely and Always

The Shattered Promises Series:

Shattered Promises

Fractured Souls

Unbroken

Broken Visions

Scattered Ashes

Breaking Nova Series:

Breaking Nova

Saving Quinton

Delilah: The Making of Red

Nova and Quinton: No Regrets

Tristan: Finding Hope

Wreck Me

Ruin Me

The Fallen Star Series:

The Fallen Star

The Underworld

The Vision

The Promise

The Lost Soul

The Evanescence

The Mist of Stars (untitled)

The Darkness Falls Series:

Darkness Falls

Darkness Breaks

Darkness Fades

The Death Collectors Series (NA and YA):

Ember X and Ember

Cinder X and Cinder

Spark X and Spark

Unbeautiful Series:

Unbeautiful

Untamed

www.ingramcontent.com/pod-product-compliance
Lightning Source LLC
Chambersburg PA
CBHW030642190726

48286CB00008B/2614